RUNNING MATES

LILA DEAR

Muse Books

RUNNING MATES

Written by Lila Dear

Published by Muse Books

Muse Books

ISBN

978-1-60020-206-3

1-60020-206-3

CONTENTS

For Finn.

CHAPTER 1

I HAVE NEVER been the biggest weeper in the world.

But, on the night that I became an old maid, got dumped by my boyfriend of five years, and lost the biggest primary election in my young career, I was bawling like a pro.

I legitimately went through two boxes of tissues, which may or may not have been a record considering I only had the thin, generic ones because I'm that cheap.

"I think we have to open some wine," my best friend, Gabby, said, trying her best to console me, though it wasn't working in the slightest.

Everything that my life had been made up of to that point had suddenly come to an abrupt, brutal end. All that was left was a losing campaign and $93k in student debt.

"All I have is champagne. For celebraaaation . . . ," I said and resumed my blubbering.

"Well . . . how about . . . ," Gabby said, scanning my cupboard. "Is this alcoholic?" she asked, holding up a bottle of absinthe.

"Jay got it on our trip to Praaaaague!" I said through more sobs.

"Ah!" she said, and quickly tossed the bottle back in the cupboard. "Ice cream?!"

Her effort was adorable and I actually managed a laugh. "I'm sorry I'm so inconsolable."

"You totally have nothing to be sorry about, Libby," she said, retrieving a pint of Haagen Dazs from my freezer. "Now, I don't want to hear apologizing from you—only crying and eating ice cream, young lady."

"You're the best," I said, and started gobbling up the ice cream.

"The way I see it," she said, putting her arm on my shoulder, "you just need to get through this little setback anyway possible because, on the other side, it'll be pretty obvious that you are brilliant, beautiful, and have the world waiting for you."

"Are you trying to make me cry even more?" I said, laughing through my tears.

* * *

"Okay, let's think about it," Gabby said, her voice taking on that fiery cadence I'd heard her use when rallying the troops during a campaign crunch. She perched on the edge of my coffee table, hands animatedly sketching the future she envisioned for me in the air. "You are a rare bird."

"Am I?"

"Crazy beautiful."

I blushed.

"Like, too gorgeous for this old town," she continued. I was in too much need of a pick-me-up to protest. "And you're pretty amazingly smart too."

I clicked my teeth and tried to play it off with a tilt of my head.

"You're too good for this place!" Gabby cheered. And then she paused and looked deep into my eyes. "You belong in D.C. with me!"

I shook my head, less because I disagreed and more because I just didn't want to think about such a big move.

"No, it makes perfect sense," she said. "D.C. is like Hollywood for nerds. You walk down K Street and it's like . . . like the Avengers of policy wonks and legislative heroes. And Libs . . . you're like the Wonder Woman of policy wonks!"

"Those are different fictional universes, Gabs."

"You get what I'm saying though."

I glanced up from my fortress of crumpled tissues, caught between a chuckle and a grimace. "I don't know if I even want to stay in politics."

"Oh no."

"It's true," I said. "I mean, we ran the cleanest, most idealistic campaign, and we still got trounced."

"Five percentage points is not getting trounced."

"If there were any justice in the world, Charlie would have *won* by five."

"See," she insisted, refusing to let the spark of hope die. "Everyone in D.C. is as policy-obsessed as you. We eat, sleep, and breathe this stuff!"

I shifted uncomfortably, tracing the patterns on my worn-out jeans. There was an undeniable allure in Gabby's vision of the city—a pulsing hive of shared ambition and intellect.

"Sure, but it's also where idealism goes to get mugged in a back alley by lobbyists," I countered, the cynicism seeping through despite myself. "You know I've always wanted to make a difference, but lately. . . . " My voice trailed off as I grappled with the thought, "It feels like I'm trying to drain the Atlantic with a teaspoon."

"But that's exactly why you need to be there. Be the change, Libs. Remind them politics can have a conscience."

"I don't know."

"Besides, you've never backed down from a challenge before. Why start now?"

"Because every time I throw a punch for justice, it's like the system grows another head?" I said, though the edges of my resolve were undeniably softening.

"Hydra references? Really?" Gabby teased, rolling her eyes. "You are such a nerd."

"Guilty," I admitted with a half-smile.

"Look, Elizabeth Hart," she said, grabbing my hands in hers, an earnest plea lacing her words, "there's a whole city out there full of people who get it. Who feel the same passion burning through their veins. People who—"

"Are probably just as messed up and lost as I am?" I interjected.

Now I was just being difficult. I didn't want to admit that a town full of kindred spirits was really comforting.

"You know what I really want?" I posed, contemplatively. "To be able to just go for a walk, holding hands with someone who knows me. Truly knows me."

"D.C., girl," Gabby shot back, her confidence unshakable.

"I can find that there?" The corners of my mouth twitched upward involuntarily. Gabby's relentless optimism was contagious, even if my heart wasn't quite ready to leap without looking again.

"One hundred percent," she affirmed, giving my hands a squeeze before finally letting go.

* * *

The room pulsed with the low murmur of commentators dissecting every percentage point and precinct, but my focus was as scattered as the remnants of my campaign flyers strewn across the coffee table.

"Would you look at that," Gabby said as she eyed a handsome politico being interviewed on television. "Isn't he something?"

"Something's one word for it."

"Come on, Libby," Gabby prodded, her eyes flickering between me and the television. "Hollywood's got nothing on this hunk."

"Sure, if you're into that whole 'I just won a marathon and solved world hunger before breakfast' vibe," I said, though a reluctant smirk played at my lips.

"Look at him," she urged again. "Now that's a reason you should come to D.C. if I ever saw one!"

"Gabby, he's clearly a Republican. Look at him! He looks like Alex P. Keaton with a five o'clock shadow."

"Don't be so quick to judge! Maybe he's a major social justice warrior who just happens to be well-groomed and totally preppy," she said. "I mean stranger things have happened."

"No chance," I shot back, pointing to the screen.

The interviewer asked about his candidate's race and he mentioned the name 'Barry George'.

"Uh huh!" I said. "That's what I thought." Barry George was the Republican incumbent in our race, and expected to win the general election easily.

"Ugh!" Gabby said. "Okay, so he's the Republicanest Republican ever, but he's still an absolute fox."

"Oh great, Gabs," I said, "not only do you have me packing up and moving across the country to D.C., but you've got me paired up with the enemy. Thanks a lot."

"Maybe he's secretly yearning for a whip-smart, devastatingly attractive Democrat strategist to show him the light."

"Or lead him into darkness, depending on your perspective," I countered, but at least there was laughter in my voice now.

"It's perfect! You can debate tax reform over candlelight, gerrymandering over breakfast . . . ."

"Scandalous," I said, the edges of my mouth creeping upward.

We paused to hear him answering questions about Barry George's challenger in the primary, a feisty woman who put up more of a fight than most had predicted.

"Well," he said, "as my father put it, 'Nothing is more thrilling than to disagree with a beautiful woman!'"

"Say what?!"

The way he so smoothly let the sexism dribble off his lips

made me want to punch him in the glasses. Even though he wasn't wearing glasses. He was everything I hated about Republicans.

And yet at the same time I felt something churn inside my chest. He was clearly sexist and bigoted and who knows what else, but strangely I don't think I had ever found anyone more attractive. This wasn't supposed to happen.

"Thank you for talking with us, William Benjamin," the interviewer said, then turned to close.

I sighed.

"Think about it, Libs. It's D.C. Where else can you find love and a filibuster all in the same day?" Gabby winked, and I couldn't help but laugh.

"Only you would find romantic potential in legislative obstruction," I said, shaking my head.

"Hey. You too, my friend, you too," she shot back, her smile wide as it was infectious.

"I'm thinking I should just stick to lobbying for heartbreak reform," I said, raising an eyebrow.

* * *

The room was still spinning with the remnants of our laughter when the familiar hum of my phone buzzing came through. I fumbled for my phone, nearly knocking over a stack of campaign flyers that had become part of the furniture over the past few months.

"Libby Hart," I answered, not bothering to check the caller ID.

"Hi, Libby. It's Malcolm Reeves here, director at Jefferson Strategies." My heart did a somersault. Jefferson Strategies was Gabby's playground, the holy grail of political consultancies in D.C.

"Malcolm! Hi." I tried to sound casual, but my voice pitched up half an octave. "What can I do for you?"

"Actually, it's what we can possibly do for each other," he said, his words as smooth as a lobbyist's handshake. "I've been following your work in the primaries. You've got a fire, Libby. I've seen it."

"You do?" I tried, stupidly. Gabby's eyes were saucers, mirroring my shock.

"We've got Kenton Peats for the general election and we'll need someone with your passion and talent to help us take down Barry George."

I was flipping in my head. This was what I had always wanted.

"Consider it an invitation to join us here in Washington," Malcolm continued. "We have an opening for a senior strategist, and I think you'd be the perfect fit."

"Senior strategist?" The title was hefty, the kind that would normally send my mind into tactical overdrive. But right now, all I could feel was the thrumming excitement, a spark reigniting within me.

"Absolutely. We require someone who's not afraid to dive into the fray, who can navigate the labyrinth of Capitol Hill with finesse—and from what I've seen, you're no stranger to a challenge."

"Wow," was all I managed, my brain short-circuiting. "This

is—"

"Do it!" Gabby chimed in, unable to contain herself any longer.

"Exactly," Malcolm agreed, chuckling. "So, what do you say, Libby? Ready for a fresh start?"

"Libby, this is it!" Gabby whispered fiercely. "Your comeback story starts now!"

"Okay, Malcolm," I said, feeling my chest swell with the first genuine spark of excitement in months. "You've got yourself a strategist."

"Brilliant!" Malcolm cheered on the other end. "Do you think you can get here by next week? We're already started on the campaign."

"Right," I said, eyeing Gabby, who was nodding exaggeratedly. "Yes, next week is doable." And we confirmed the details before hanging up.

Once I did, I paused to take in all that had just happened.

"Well Gabs," I said, glancing at her with a smile, "looks like you've got a new partner in crime." Gabby was already up and dancing in celebration.

"This is going to be epic," she said.

I just smiled and nodded. Who knew if it would be a fairytale ending, but it was a beginning, and, for the first time in what felt like forever, that was more than enough.

CHAPTER 2

I WAS A kid the last time I had been to D.C. on a junior high school trip. But I had been too wrapped up in the demands of school work and who was crushing on who to realize all that I was seeing.

Now I was there as a twenty-five-year-old and I felt more childlike than I was the first time, marveling at all the stately buildings and museums and monuments. As soon as I arrived, I set out for a tour of the National Mall, and did everything I could to glimpse every single notable attraction along that glorious stretch.

But I felt that it was more than a hokey tourist jaunt. It was a pilgrimage. With each step, I felt myself drawn deeper into the heart of the city and the soul of this country. The town was more than just a geographical location—it was a living embodiment of America's values and aspirations. And, as I encountered Washington, Jefferson, Lincoln, and Roosevelt, their words and deeds scrawled out on marble resonated in a way that I can't imagine any religious text could.

It was at the Lincoln Memorial, as I sat on the cold stone

stairs, looking back over the Reflecting Pool and the Washington Monument and Capitol in the distance as the setting sun threw golden light over the landscape, that I began to realize that I was destined to live there. What had seemed so scary a move suddenly became a no-brainer in my mind. This was where I was meant to be—among the history and ideals. The campaign was just an excuse to be there. This was the real reason.

I strolled to my apartment at a leisurely pace, partly because I was exhausted after twelve straight hours of sightseeing, but also because I didn't want to let go of that feeling of connection, purpose. Of course, I realized, all good things come to an end. And I had to get home and rest up for my first day with the campaign.

* * *

Though I was exhausted from the long day of touring, I got up at dawn so I could go for a run along the Mall. It was a dream to be living there, so I figured I would make the most of it.

I showered and assembled my sharpest skirt suit. I wanted to make a hell of a first impression. The moment I stepped into the campaign office, it was like walking onto the set of a political thriller—only the drama was real and the stakes were much higher than ratings. The hum of fervent discussions reverberated off the walls, a symphony of ideals and ambition that could either harmonize beautifully or clash spectacularly.

There was no receptionist, so I stood there, looking around at the people rushing back and forth, hoping that someone would notice my out-of-place body.

"Libby Hart?" A voice cut through the cacophony, and I turned to see a man with a crunchy smile to match his crunchy cargo shorts. "Malcolm Reeves, it's great to meet you in person."

"Glad to meet you as well," I said, reaching out for a handshake. "I was just about ready to start stacking flyers."

"No need to do that yet," he creaked, "but maybe later."

"Just let me know," I said, laughing.

"Come on," he said with a wave toward the commotion, "I'll show you around."

"Over here we've got our policy wonks," he said, gesturing toward a group crowded around several whiteboards covered in a tangle of notes and diagrams. "And there's our digital team— they're wizards with social media algorithms. The lawyers are back there. And finally, the interns. Eager, caffeinated, and occasionally right about something."

"Sounds like a potent mix," I observed, feeling the pulse of the place seep into my veins.

"Potent is one word for it," he agreed.

Still buzzing with the energy of the bustling campaign office, I followed Malcolm as he led me through the chaotic sea of dedicated staff members. As we weaved through the maze of passionate politicos, my eyes caught a flash of movement near the entrance. A figure strode in with an air of authority that demanded attention. She was like a fierce storm rolling in, each step echoing power and determination. Her sleek black hair shone under the bright office lights, and her sharp brown eyes seemed to pierce through everything in her path.

"Who's that?" I whispered to Malcolm, unable to tear my gaze away from this force of nature.

Malcolm glanced over at the woman who was now barking orders at someone, her tone leaving no room for negotiation. "That's Vanessa Martinez, our senior consultant," he replied, a hint of caution in his voice. "Let's just say you'd better hope you don't end up on her bad side."

Vanessa Martinez disappeared into her office, her presence leaving an indelible imprint on the buzzing campaign office. As I tried to shake off the overwhelming aura she exuded, Malcolm led me towards a group of staffers huddled around a conference table covered with maps and data projections.

"All right, Libby, ready to dive in?" Malcolm asked after a brisk tour. "We've got a mountain of work and only so many hours before the next news cycle tries to bury us."

"Absolutely," I replied, my determination matching Malcolm's urgency. As we delved into the heart of the campaign headquarters, I couldn't help but feel a surge of adrenaline at the prospect of contributing to something so significant. Images of policy papers, canvassing routes, and social media campaigns swirled in my mind, each contributing to the greater cause.

Malcolm led me to a cluttered corner where stacks of papers threatened to topple over. "This," he said with a wry smile, "is where the magic happens. We need all these files sorted, categorized, and digitized by tomorrow morning. Think you can handle it?"

I nodded, rolling up my sleeves metaphorically as I prepared to tackle the mundane task with gusto. The sun sliced through the campaign windows, lighting the office with columns of fire, as I immersed myself in the world of campaign data entry. Every rustle of paper and tap of the keyboard felt like a step closer to understanding the intricate dance of political strategy.

As I methodically worked through the piles of papers, organizing and inputting data with precision, the energy of the bustling office enveloped me. The digital team's laughter floated across the room, mixing with the intense discussions of the policy wonks. My campaign back in Indiana was amateur compared to this. This was the prime time.

Just as I was getting engrossed in my task, Gabby breezed into the office, her bright smile cutting through the serious air. "Libby!" she exclaimed, causing heads to turn in our direction. "How's your first day going?"

I looked up from my work, a mix of exhaustion and excitement twinkling in my eyes. "Gabby, it's been incredible! I feel like I've found my tribe here," I replied, gesturing at the chaos around us with a sense of belonging.

"I had a feeling," Gabby cheered, her eyes scanning the room before landing back on me. "Hey, so, drinks tonight at Clifton's?"

I gave Gabby an exaggerated nod and smiled. "Exactly what I'll need after this."

"Okay," Gabby exclaimed, "I'll swing by around five."

"Thanks, chickie," I said, and dove back into my papers.

* * *

The hum of huddled conversations and the clatter of keyboards were like a symphony to my racing heart, each note propelling me further into the political fray. I was in my element, firing off emails with the precision of a seasoned pro, my fingers dancing across the keys in a rhythmic manifesto of ambition.

As I continued to immerse myself in the piles of campaign data, intent on organizing it all by the looming deadline, the familiar sound of sharp heels clicking against the office floor announced Vanessa's approach. I braced myself internally, steeling against her impending presence as she came closer.

I couldn't help but overhear bits of her conversation with Malcolm as they neared my corner of the office. "Malcolm, this is unacceptable. We cannot afford to waste time on these minor details. I need those projections finalized yesterday," Vanessa's voice dripped with impatience and disdain.

Malcolm shot me a sympathetic look before redirecting Vanessa's attention elsewhere. But before long, Vanessa had turned her gaze towards me, her sharp brown eyes cutting through the room as she demanded, "Are you the new intern?"

"This is Libby Hart, our new senior strategist," Malcolm said, but Vanessa didn't seem to care.

"What's taking so long?" she said, barging into my space.

Frozen under her intense scrutiny, I fumbled to explain my progress, trying to show her the meticulous work I was doing to contribute to the campaign strategy. But Vanessa's face twisted into a scowl, unimpressed by my explanation. "This isn't the way to get ahead in this business, Libby. You're playing 2D chess—we play 3D chess here," she bellowed, her tone making it clear that she had no patience for anything less than perfection.

Feeling the pressure mounting, I attempted to defend my method, "I believe that attention to detail is crucial in ensuring accuracy and reliability in our data. It may take a little longer, but—"

Vanessa cut me off with a dismissive wave of her hand. "I don't have time for your excuses. If you want to be senior strategist here, you'd better learn how we do things," she snapped, her words like icicles piercing through the warmth of the office atmosphere.

Malcolm, sensing the tension escalating, attempted to intervene diplomatically. "Vanessa, perhaps—"

But Vanessa was having none of it. With a frustrated huff, she turned on her heel and stormed off in a swirl of tailored fabric and self-righteousness.

Malcolm moaned. "Eh, don't let her get to you," he said. "She's a little tightly wound."

"3D chess?" I inquired.

"Yeah, one of her favorites," Malcolm said. "Imagine you're playing your regular game of chess on an eight-by-eight board. That's 2Ds."

"Okay."

"Now imagine you're playing that *and* another vertical board at the same time. 3D chess."

"Got it."

"Do you think we can have these by the end of the day?" Malcolm tried.

I looked down at my stack of papers and nodded. Then I got back to work.

As the clock mercilessly ticked closer to the 5 p.m. deadline, I kicked into overdrive, channeling all my frustration and determination into the task at hand. Every keystroke felt like a battle won, every document organized a victory in the making. With each passing minute, the symphony of the office transformed into a cacophony of urgency, driving me to push myself harder, faster.

And, just before the clock hit five, I completed my final input. I stacked the papers and went over to Malcolm's desk to deliver.

"You are amazing," he said, looking somewhat surprised that I had gotten it all done.

"Want me to go deliver to the boss lady?"

"No," he said, "you get out of here before she remembers we exist."

"Thanks, Malcolm."

"I'm sorry you had to deal with it so soon," he said.

I offered him a reassuring smile, brushing off Vanessa's behavior as just another obstacle to overcome. "No worries, Malcolm. It's all part of the game," I replied with a forced nonchalance, masking the storm brewing beneath my composed exterior.

Gabby's cheerful voice broke through the tension as she flew into the office right on time. "Are you overworking this girl on her first day?" she asked Malcolm as she linked her arm with mine.

"Someone switched the goalposts," Malcolm said, tilting his head in the direction of Vanessa's office.

"I could have guessed," Gabby sighed. "You okay?"

"Oh yeah," I said. "I knew it was going to be different here."

"Not quite the Midwestern hospitality that you're used to?" Gabby jabbed.

"No, they don't prepare us like they do in New York," I said, referencing Gabby's home town.

"It's different," she said. "New York is a tough town. Washington is a *mean* town."

"Yeah, I'm learning that."

"Well, let's get out of here before she makes you block walk Anacostia," Gabby said.

We all laughed, but something told me it wasn't outside the realm of possibility.

Gabby and I offered a wave to Malcolm and in a flash we were gone.

CHAPTER 3

GLASSES CLINKED, REHAB to my frazzled nerves. Gabby's smile was a sparkling Lambrusco in a sea of tap water faces. "To surviving Day One," she cheered, and our glasses kissed with promise.

"Ugh, I swear Vanessa's glare could laser-print her memos," Gabby winced, swirling the wine in her glass.

"Hey, if looks could legislate," I chirped, tipping the glass to my lips. "We'd have health care reform by morning." Secretly, I thought that Vanessa's shark-in-a-blazer vibe had its appeal. I had been raised to appreciate work ethic and ambition. And she was the embodiment of those virtues.

"Whoa! Party favors!" a wild voice sliced through the barroom buzz as a vivacious blond materialized at our corner of the bar, her grin armed and dangerous. Shots lined up on the table like soldiers on parade, courtesy of the bombshell who never met a happy hour she couldn't hijack.

"Libby Hart, prepare to be shocked and awed," Gabby said. "The one and only Amanda Peters, legal council by day, life of the party by night."

Without so much as a handshake, Amanda thrust a shot into my hand. The tequila smelled like a challenge.

"Is it even legal to serve these without a splash zone?" I joked, raising an eyebrow.

"Only one way to find out," Amanda winked, throwing back her shot with gusto.

"Speaking of campaigns," she began, swiping a napkin across her lips, "which one of these suits is going to be on my bathroom floor tonight?" Her gaze prowled the room, lioness on the hunt, sizing up the Capitol Hill gazelles that grazed around us.

I just watched the girl wide-eyed and hoped I wouldn't get in her way.

* * *

The air was electric with political gossip and the scent of ambition, but Amanda's hunt for a legislative Lothario had my stomach twisting.

"Come on, Libs," Gabby said, leaning in. "You've been out of the game since, what . . . ?"

"Since Jay decided his intern was more . . . intern-esting," I finished for her, the bitterness still fresh.

"Exactly," Gabby said, squeezing my hand gently. "But you can't let that stop you from jumping back in."

"Let me guess," I said, "there are plenty of fish in the D.C. swamp?"

"That's the spirit!" Gabby cheered.

"I don't know if I fit the whole swipe-right scene," I said.

"More for me," Amanda said, actually lifting her phone and taking a selfie as we talked.

"You're not looking for a life-long partner?" I asked.

"'Life-long partner'?" she shot back. "What is this, Dr. Phil?"

"No, you're right, that sounds so old fashioned," I said, shrugging.

"Here's the deal," Amanda said, suddenly serious. "I know my place. You two have a chance at Prince Charming, but I'd be fighting a losing battle."

"Why do you say that?" I asked.

"Look, there's a formula to all this madness."

"Enlighten us, oh wise one," Gabby said, skeptical.

"Good guys—the marrying kind—they want three main things in a woman: looks, brains, and money." Amanda counted off on her fingers.

"Now, they realize that having all three is like finding a unicorn—they don't exist. So they don't even bother looking for them. They want a girl who has at least two of the big three. If she has looks and money—marriable. Looks and brains? Marriable. Brains and money? Marriable. If a girl has none of them, she basically doesn't exist."

I hummed. "What if she has one of the three?"

"Cuddle buddy," she said.

"Is that what you call it now?!"

"Believe me, that's where I fall," Amanda said. "If you have brains but no money or looks, good guys will hook up with you but there's no chance they'll put a ring on it."

"Get out of here!"

"Think about it. What about a girl who's attractive but doesn't have brains or money? Cuddle buddy."

I nodded, beginning to see her logic.

"Trust me I know because that's exactly where I am. I've got brains—too much considering the level of intellect in most of the guys I've met. But no money—hello, I'm in politics. And no looks."

"Stop it," I protested, rolling my eyes. "You could torch the Inaugural Ball with that body."

"Smoke and mirrors, Libby, smoke and mirrors." Amanda laughed hollowly. "Gabby here, she's the unicorn. Beauty, brains, and bucks."

"Hey now, don't use me to prove your twisted conspiracy theories," Gabby waved dismissively, though a flush of pride painted her cheeks.

"Okay, so say, hypothetically, I entertain this big-three concept," I mused, feeling the tequila's warmth embolden my thoughts. "Where does that leave me?"

"Oh, you're set" Amanda exclaimed. "You've got this whole Jackie Kennedy appeal going and you're clearly smart because you're friends with Gabby. Do you have money?"

"I barely have 1k, let alone 401k," I said, shaking my head.

"Got it," Amanda concluded. "Who needs money when you're dismantling political opponents with a single word? That's priceless."

"Great, so I'm a broke brainiac with decent bone structure," I said, half-joking. "But who's the lucky guy in this fantasy equation?"

"Someone worthy of you," Gabby affirmed with a nod. "And definitely not found at the bottom of a shot glass."

"More's the pity," Amanda sighed theatrically. "Shot glasses are so much easier to find than good men."

"Cheers to that," I raised my empty glass, the irony not lost on me as we clinked our way through another round of laughter and sarcasm.

* * *

The bar was a melting pot of tailored suits and political prowess, each man seemingly vying for the title of Capitol Hill's Most Eligible Douche. Amanda's eyes darted around like a Secret Service agent scoping for threats—or, in her case, targets.

"Libby, there are so many options here it's like a political Tinder," Amanda said, winking at a young aide who blushed under her gaze.

"Easy for you to say," I replied, taking a sip of my drink and trying not to look interested in the game she was playing.

"Wait, isn't that. . . . " Gabby's voice trailed off as she nudged me, nodding toward a group across the room. "William Benjamin?"

My head shot up and my eyes scanned where she was looking. There he was, the Republican golden boy with a jawline sharp enough to slice through gridlock. William Benjamin, his crown of hair impeccably styled, stood laughing among a gang of navy-suited tetrarchs, a whiskey glass poised in his hand like a scepter.

"Go talk to him," Gabby urged, practically shoving me out of my seat.

"Are you delusional?" I scoffed. "He's on the wrong side of the aisle. Like right-hand-man-to-Senator-Barry-George wrong."

"Who cares?" Amanda cut in, her eyes shining with mischief. "He's hot—like Climate-Change-is-real hot."

"She's right," Gabby chimed.

Amanda started dancing to Salt-N-Pepa even though Salt-N-Pepa weren't playing. "OMG, he's so hot. I would totally swoon over him if I did that sort of thing."

"Even if I were interested—which I'm not—guys like him are players. He's probably got a Rolodex just for floozies he's met at Clifton's." The bitterness in my voice surprised even me.

"Which is why . . . ," Gabby started, her eyes dancing with excitement, "we'll send Amanda!"

Amanda twisted her face. "Uh, this isn't going to fetch that hunk, I can tell you right now."

"No, no, no," Gabby said. "You're playing 2D chess. We need to go at least 3D here."

"What am I missing?" Amanda said.

"Okay," Gabby said, leaning in, "Amanda goes and tries to bag him. If he goes for her, well, then, good for Amanda. But, if he doesn't . . . ."

"Then he might be good enough for Libby," Amanda cheered as she connected the dots.

"You don't mind, do you Man-hands?" Gabby asked.

"Not a bit. I'll be the canary in the carnal coal mine," Amanda declared, her confidence unshaken. "If he's a player, he won't resist me. If he does, then he's all yours."

"Because nothing says romance like being some girl's sloppy seconds," I muttered, but the adventurous part of me was perversely intrigued by the plan.

"Stop overthinking it, Libby," Amanda chastised, fixing a lock of her hair with a practiced twist. "He's too good to pass up. Plus, think of the scandal it could bring!"

Before I could protest further, Amanda sauntered into the crowd, leaving Gabby and me in a bubble of anticipation. Watching her weave through the throng of politicos, I couldn't help but wonder what kind of man this William Benjamin truly was. My heart thrummed a nervous beat. This was either going to be a hilarious disaster or the start of something dangerously exciting.

* * *

I angled my wine glass just so, pretending to be absorbed in the swirl of ruby liquid while sneakily tracking Amanda's beeline toward William Benjamin. Gabby, ever the co-conspirator, nudged me under the bar—a silent signal that the show was on.

"Is it just me, or is she laying it on thicker than the foundation at a beauty pageant?" I whispered out of the corner of my mouth, my eyes fixated on the way Amanda flipped her hair with the precision of a seasoned flirt.

"Girl could teach masterclasses," Gabby murmured back, her elbow discreetly jutting into my side as she leaned forward to get a better look. "I don't know if he's going to crack."

"Please, he'll fold faster than Superman on laundry day." The words tumbled out before I could stop them. A part of me—probably the one not nursing a fresh break-up wound—was curious if this William Benjamin had more substance than his starched shirt suggested.

Amanda was all sizzle and sass, touching William's arm in a way that seemed casual but screamed intention. His face, however, was an unreadable mask: polite interest painted over a politician's poker face. I couldn't tell if he was intrigued or merely tolerating her advances for the sake of public decorum.

"God, I hope he's not into her act," I admitted, the sour twist in my stomach betraying my cool exterior. And why did I care again? Oh, right, because apparently I'm now in high school, passing notes and sending friends to do my dirty work.

"Is that a touch of concern," Gabby chuckled. "Maybe there's hope for bipartisan romance yet."

"Or the apocalypse," I countered. "Equally likely at this point."

Our banter was cut short by a server who bounced up with enough energy to power the Washington Monument. "More wine for the lovely ladies?" he sang, oblivious to the covert operation we were running from our corner. "Or tequila?"

"Wine, yes, no more tequila, friend," Gabby replied, flashing him a grin that might have encouraged further conversation under different circumstances.

"Fantastic choice! Might I say that this pinot noir is like a hug for your taste buds?!" he gushed, pouring with a flourish that would have been impressive if I weren't desperately trying to crane my neck around him to keep visuals on Amanda and William.

"You might," I said through gritted teeth, aiming for politeness but probably landing somewhere closer to 'get lost'.

As soon as he scampered off, I whipped back around, only to find the space where Amanda and Will stood conspicuously empty. No sign of the political Adonis or our femme fatale.

"Damn," I muttered, scanning the room frantically. "They're gone."

"Did they leave together, or did he duck and cover?" Gabby wondered aloud, her gaze darting across the bustling crowd.

I just hummed to myself.

"Knowing Amanda, she's probably giving him a personal tour of Ford's Theater," she said, half-joking but fully dreading the answer.

"Or maybe he's a gentleman, and they're just grabbing a quieter drink," I offered, hoping the best for Amanda.

I took a hearty swig of the newly poured wine, bracing myself for whatever came next in this romantic comedy of errors.

CHAPTER 4

"WELL THAT DIDN'T go as planned!" Amanda said, slinking back against the bar, startling both Gabby and me.

"What happened?" Gabby asked as I tried to act disinterested.

"Oh you know, a little quickie in the women's bathroom," Amanda said, touching up her lipstick.

Gabby and I stared at her with jaws dropped.

"What?" she asked, and then laughed. "I'm totally joking, you two."

I released a breath so big it could have blown out birthday candles.

"I mean, did you see that?" she asked, trying to play off her embarrassment. "He didn't even flinch. I swear, he's either got the willpower of a saint or he's a eunuch."

"Or maybe he's just not that into you," I posed, my heartbeat settling back into its regular rhythm now that I knew William hadn't fallen for Amanda's charms.

"Libs, if he can say no to this," she said, circling her hand around her bosom as if she were showcasing a prize on a game show, "he's definitely more your speed. You should go talk to him."

"I don't know—if you couldn't entice him . . . ." I tried to keep my voice light, but the idea of wading across the partisan waters to this William guy had my stomach doing flips.

"Come on, Libby. He's hot, you're hot—it's like bipartisan sexy time waiting to happen." Amanda nudged me forward, nearly spilling my drink.

"Sexy time?" I snorted, shaking my head. "What are we, in junior high?"

"Fine, call it 'crossing the aisle for a little horizontal diplomacy.'" Amanda winked. "Either way, it's scandalous, and I'm here for it."

"Scandalous is one word for it," I muttered. I was definitely over Jay, but I didn't think I was ready for another relationship, especially one that seemed like it would be such a challenge. I didn't have to work for Jay. Then again, maybe that was the problem.

"Think of it as . . . engaging in some undercover research," Amanda said, nudging me again. "Or under *covers* research. You decide."

"Under covers?!" I echoed, arching an eyebrow. "Is this a James Bond movie?"

"More like James Bod," she teased.

"Girl," I said, half-heartedly scanning the room, pretending I wasn't trying to locate William again.

"Well," Amanda sighed, "while you two are strategerizing, I'm going to the ladies' room."

Gabby said she had to go as well, and I shook my head no.

"Someone's got to keep our chatty waiter company," I said as the girls sashayed toward the restrooms.

* * *

I was flipping through my messages when I sensed a man taking Gabby's stool and a voice say, "Red or blue?"

"Excuse me?" I prompted before looking up to see that it was none other than William Benjamin.

"Red or blue?" he repeated. "You know, trickle down or tax and spend? Bootstraps or it takes a village?"

I couldn't help but to laugh.

"Republican or Democrat?" he clarified.

I nodded, acting as if it made any more sense. "Do you work for Gallup or something?" I retorted, trying to match his cool composure while my mind raced.

"Something," he said, grinning. "I'm not used to picking up girls, but my friend says that, in D.C., you have to ask for affiliation before you talk to anyone."

"Doesn't that seem rather limiting?"

"How so?"

"I mean, you might have a real interest in someone and not be able to talk with her just because she's on the other side," I reasoned. "Wouldn't it be much better to talk about the arts or something?"

"Well, possibly," he said. "But what if you get to know someone and like him a lot, but after getting ultra-invested you find out that he's a lunatic?"

"Yeah, you've got a point," I said, shrugging.

"The former is much easier," he said, his smile widening.

"Are you a hardliner on this matter?"

He shrugged. "We are in D.C. after all."

"So we are," I said, nervously bouncing my foot, and studying his face. He was so playful about it, even sweet. I couldn't imagine this was the same guy who was heading up Barry George's campaign. But there he was.

"Reeedd . . . ," I let ease out across several syllables, and then watched his expression. He actually seemed elated, as if he had just passed the big test. And, when I saw that, I felt like I had passed the test too.

"Okay, so now we can talk about the arts," he said.

"Are you really interested in it?"

"Well, I should qualify," he said, "real art. Not this garbage they're putting out there in contemporary art museums."

"What, you aren't a fan of 'Detached Urinal No. 9'?"

"Not my favorite."

"What about the banana taped to the wall?"

"I've seen more beautiful car repair shop lobbies."

"Ouch," I said, laughing.

"I'm William," he said, reaching out for a handshake.

"Pleased to meet you. I'm Elizabeth." I don't know why I told him that. I hadn't been called 'Elizabeth' since the first grade. It just came out. Maybe I was trying to hide my real identity. Maybe I wanted to match his British royal-sounding name. Either way, it was weird, like I was becoming someone different just by talking with him.

"Hey, so, was that your friend who cornered me before?" he asked, gesturing to where Amanda accosted him.

"Oh, Amanda," I said, "she's harmless."

"She tried to sit on my lap when I was standing up."

I tittered. "She's quite a woman, no?" Now I was testing him.

"She seemed rather . . . determined."

"Oh, she'll get her way in life."

"Well, more power to her," he said.

"She's not your type?" I prompted.

He shook his head. "No, I'd much prefer an evening stroll on the National Mall, holding hands with someone who really knows me."

When he said it, I shot an intense glance at him, trying to figure out if he was answering honestly or if he had been tipped to my dream date and was setting me up.

"I know it sounds hokey, but I think it's one of the most romantic things—walking together through all the history and ideas and ideals."

Could it possibly be that this man was for real? Surely Gabby put him up to this somehow.

"It is quite a town," I said, totally hiding the fact that I wanted to jump on his lap and start kissing him right there.

"I've been in D.C. for years and I still can't get over how majestic it is." He was leaning toward me as if to see if I approved. "Are you new here?"

"I just moved here this week."

"What do you think?"

"Pretty majestic," I conceded with a smile.

The clatter of heels on polished marble punctuated the roar of conversation as Gabby and Amanda returned and stopped abruptly when they saw who I was talking to.

Gabby's wild curls did a somersault she was so taken aback. "Well, hello friends," she said, easing back into our space at the bar.

"Gabby and Amanda, this is William," I said, my voice steady despite the sudden urge to hyperventilate into a paper bag. "William, Gabby's my best friend from forever ago, and Amanda's . . . well, you've already met Amanda."

"Not formerly," he offered, his smile easy as he shook their hands.

"Charmed," Gabby beamed.

"Well, I'm just surprised," Amanda said playfully, "that you two would hit it off."

"Why surprised?"

"Well, you're, you know, such a . . . ," she began.

"Monument nerd!" I blurted out, a touch too loudly, cutting her off mid-sentence. My heart hammered against my ribs like it was trying to get out and slap Amanda for almost ruining it. "Turns out, Mister William here is a fan of the monuments as well." I said it pointedly so that Amanda would catch the drift.

"Oh," Amanda said, puzzled.

"We were just about to go for a walk. Right, William?"

"Uh, yes, The National Mall beckons." His response came swift and sure, a lifeline thrown with impeccable precision.

"The Mall?" Gabby asked, casting me a knowing look that meant we'd be dissecting this interaction later over wine and gluten-free cookies.

Amanda opened her mouth, no doubt ready to spill more than just the beans, but I looped my arm through William's before she could divulge the minefield of my political life.

"Lead the way, sir," I teased, guiding us toward the nearest exit with the finesse of a seasoned diplomat dodging a presser.

With one last look at my friends, who still wore matching expressions of disbelief, I whisked William Benjamin away into the Washington night, where the only party lines drawn would be in the stars above us.

CHAPTER 5

WILLIAM BENJAMIN AND I tumbled out of the bar and I set a quick pace down 23rd Street toward the Lincoln Monument. I was partly relieved to escape the Amanda situation and partly excited to see the monuments again. Truth be told, I was also very nervous to be walking with quite possibly the most handsome man in D.C.

"Thanks for playing along back there," I said, sidestepping a crowd of lollygaggers.

"Hey, I'm here to help," William shot back, hands tucked in his pockets like he didn't have a care in the world.

"Gabby is great," I mused. "Amanda . . . she seems like quite a handful."

"So I gathered," he said, and his glance held a universe of untold stories.

Once we reached the Mall, we slowed down to take in the vision of monuments and cherry blossoms in full bloom. William nodded toward the seated figure etched against the Western horizon.

"Every time it gets me," he said, his childlike awe unmistakable.

"It's even better going for a run along here," I noted.

He looked at me askance. "You run?"

"I try to keep up."

"I bet," he said, tilting his head as if to assess my gait. "We'll, if you need a running mate for . . . running, you know who to call."

I smiled at the thought. Of course the competitive spirit in me wondered if he could keep up with me.

"Did you ever notice how Lincoln looks like he is keeping an eye on Congress from over there?" he asked.

"Doesn't seem to be doing much good, does it?" I said. We shared a laugh, the sound mingling with the distant chatter of lingering tourists.

"It's all part of the game," he said with a wry grin.

I shot him a sideways glance. "So, are you in politics?"

"Isn't everyone?" he fired back, eyes twinkling with mischief, as we turned to walk along the Reflecting Pool.

"Going to be President one day?" I teased, but I was halfway serious; the man had gravitas.

"Hard pass," he chuckled, shaking his head. "I prefer the behind-the-scenes action. You can be yourself. Once you are a politician, you have to wear a mask."

His words struck me like a bell, reminding me of the game I was playing. "I can relate," I admitted, almost ready to tell him I wasn't actually a Republican.

"What about you? Am I talking to the future Madam President?" He threw the question like a curve ball.

"Ha! Nope." I shook my head, the idea fluttering away like a startled pigeon. "I love the strategy of politics, the sociology, but. . . . " My voice trailed off as I searched for the right way to phrase the gnawing doubt that always lurked within me. "I don't know if I could handle the constant scrutiny of being a politician. Being under the microscope twenty-four, seven? Judged by everyone? No thanks."

"Yeah," William conceded, his gaze suggesting he understood more than he let on.

"Plus," I added, flashing a grin as we navigated through the throng of people, "I probably would go bonkers having to smile through those never-ending state dinners."

"But, hey, you've got a great smile," he said with a grin of his own.

I tried to gauge if he was being sincere or if this was just another hook-up campaign promise.

"Maybe you can be my running mate for *not* being president, then," he said.

"You have a deal," I said with a giggle.

* * *

"So, now that you know how to meet people in D.C.," William began, slanting a knowing smile my way, "I'll tell you how to get to know them better."

"Pray tell," I said with a smile.

"In D.C., you get to know people by who their favorite and least favorite presidents are."

"Ooh," I said, grinning enough to stall. "Good one."

"You can tell a lot about a person, you know."

"No doubt," I said.

I just about told him 'Thomas Jefferson', the words almost automatic, before I caught myself and decided to go with a more Republican figure. "I'm leaning toward Lincoln these days."

"Lincoln?" Will arched a playful eyebrow, a spark of interest lighting up his eyes. "Used to be my answer, too. But lately, I've been learning more about Jefferson. He really represents something special, don't you think?"

"Jefferson?" I retorted with mock surprise, teasing out the corner of my mouth into an impish grin. "And here I thought you were a die-hard Republican."

"Isn't it crazy?" he fired back, the lightness in his tone belying the depth of the conversation. "The first Democrat was more akin to current Republicans, and the first Republican was more like today's Democrats."

"Ah, the great switcheroo," I mused aloud, reflecting on the political contortions that had shaped our nation's history as we made our way down the Reflecting Pool.

"So, do you consider yourself conservative, then?" I asked him, unable to resist poking at the boundaries of his political persona.

"Of course, aren't you?" His response came quick as a whip crack, and he gave me a sideways glance that was nothing short of challenging.

"Well yeah, I mean, as a Republican, it's mandatory, right?" I tried. "But are you like conservative, conservative?" I pressed on, my curiosity piqued by his nonchalance.

He chuckled softly, an echo of amusement in the open night air. "Elizabeth, I'm the most conservative man you know."

So confident, almost smug. I would have slapped him if I hadn't been pretending to be a conservative myself in order to spend more time with him.

"See, that's where you throw me off," I said, the words tumbling out with a mix of skepticism and admiration. "Most conservative guys I've met are complete troglodytes. But you're different—you're really smart."

"Smart and funny," he stipulated.

"Oh yes, smart and funny."

"Well, you're not like most conservative girls I know."

"Am I smart and funny too?"

"Smart and beautiful."

Heat crept into my cheeks at the compliment, unbidden and unexpected. It was a dance of words between us, and I found myself both leading and being led in turns.

As we neared the Washington Monument, its iconic form towered over us larger and more majestic lit up with light from the setting sun. The amber hues of twilight bathed the surrounding structures in a warm glow, turning the cherry blossoms into a delicate pink oasis in the heart of the city.

* * *

"All right then, Mr. Conservative, Conservative," I said, eager to keep the verbal volleys going. "Who's your pick for worst president?"

"Definitely Johnson," he replied without missing a beat.

"Andrew Johnson was pretty bad," I agreed, recalling the grievances against the man who fumbled Reconstruction.

"No, no, Lyndon Baines," he corrected me, his tone taking on an edge.

"Really?" I arched an eyebrow, surprised at his vehemence. "But Civil Rights . . . ."

"Sure, he passed Civil Rights, but that was all a front. He was as racist as they came. Even Texans couldn't stand him."

"I find that hard to believe."

"It's true," he cut in, his voice dropping to a conspiratorial whisper. "I once spoke to a lady whose mother used to nanny LBJ. She said, 'If I'd have known what kind of a SOB he turned out to be, I would have dropped him on his head.'"

"Ouch," I remarked, though I couldn't stifle a giggle at the imagery.

"Yep," he continued, imitating the woman's Southern drawl, "'But you voted for him.' And she said, 'Yeah, I voted for him. He's an SOB, all right, but he's our SOB!'"

I watched William's face, searching for the typical signs of partisanship or bull-headedness, but all I found was an easy-going charm and wit that I hadn't seen in anyone I had met before, let alone a Republican. It seemed there was much more to this William Benjamin than met the eye, a thought that both intrigued and unnerved me in equal measure.

"That's politics for you," I said, feeling the weight of every word.

"Yeah, I hate it," he confessed, his voice low and smooth as velvet. "But I also can't get enough."

"I'm getting that sense as well," I conceded, the corners of my lips curling upwards despite myself.

As we laughed, the Capitol loomed ahead, its dome a silent sentinel against the starry sky. Soon enough, we arrived at a brownstone that oozed character and history, an accent on a town full of character and history.

"This is me," William said, gesturing to the building with a hint of pride.

"Your apartment?" I asked, lifting my eyebrows in apprecia-tion of the elegant architecture.

"Indeed." He took a step closer, his eyes locking onto mine. "Would you like to come in?"

The invitation hung in the air between us, charged with electricity and temptation. I hesitated, wondering why any woman would simply walk into a strange man's apartment. Of course, I was no typical woman, and this was no typical strange man.

"How do I know you're not a serial killer?" I posed.

"Well," he said, "I promise."

"That's just what a serial killer would say."

"You're just going to have to take a chance, then."

Really, the slight resistance was just a show. I was so caught up in the whirlwind of our banter and the unexpected connec-tion that seemed to spark whenever our gazes met that I had every intention of taking him up on his offer.

"Sure," I found myself saying, the word slipping out almost against my will. "Lead the way, Mr. Conservative, Conservative."

"Ah, after you, Miss Future Madam President," he teased, opening the door with a flourish.

CHAPTER 6

AS SOON AS I crossed the threshold of William's apartment, a cocktail of nerves and anticipation fizzed through my veins.

"Can I offer you a drink?" he asked, his voice smooth as top-shelf whiskey.

"Sure, whatever you're having," I replied, trying to keep my cool as I took in the grandeur of his living space.

The apartment was like a page torn out of a fin du siècle Architectural Digest, with high ceilings that seemed to reach for the sky and intricate crown moldings that made a girl want to curtsy. The walls were adorned with real paintings, each one telling a story of sophistication and refinement. The furniture was almost like art in itself, delicately crafted as if by hand.

"You know," he said, starting the drinks, "you can tell the quality of a bartender by the quality of his old fashioned."

"I'm an excellent judge of old fashioneds," I said.

I strolled into the parlor to see an elegant chandelier hanging from the ceiling, casting a warm glow over the room and adding a dazzling display of old-world charm.

"That's Martin Van Buren's chandelier," he noted from the

bar.

"Of course you have Martin Van Buren's chandelier in your townhouse," I said, shaking my head.

My gaze drifted around the room, landing on an expansive bookshelf that was any bibliophile's dream. The spines of political biographies nestled against classic literature, an intellectual mosaic that made my heart skip.

"You know, you can tell the quality of a man's intellect by the quality of his library," I commented.

"Judge away," he said.

"Oh I'll judge," I said nonchalantly, as though I was not about to cry at how amazing this man seemed to be. "And here I thought you only read opinion polls."

"Ah, Elizabeth, so much to learn, so much to learn." His eyes twinkled with mischief as he stirred the drinks behind the bar.

"So I've gathered," I said, stealing his line as I continued to scan his bookshelves.

He brought the drinks over and handed me one. I wasn't accustomed to taking drinks from strangers. After all, it could have been laced with any number of nefarious things and he could have had any number of nefarious plans for me. But something about him made it seem like I knew him and he wouldn't do a thing to hurt me. Or, I thought as adrenaline rushed through my veins, I was so unbelievably attracted to the man that I wouldn't mind it even if he did. Damned Republican.

Taking a sip, a drop splashed on my lip. So I licked it off. "You must be a hell of a bartender."

"You approve of my old fashioned cocktail?"

"The best thing my tongue has tasted this evening," I said, breathily. I was even surprising myself at how much I was turning on the heat. But, with him it seemed like the most natural thing to do.

I took another sip, which turned into a full drink, the warmth from the drink coursing through me, emboldening me more. Our eyes locked, and in that moment, it felt like the world around us faded into a blur of muted colors. The tension crackling between us was palpable, as though every breath we took drew us closer together.

"So, Mr. Old-Fashioned," I said with suspicion, "what's the catch?"

He just smiled and shook his head.

"I mean, someone as handsome as you, amazing library, Martin Van Buren's chandelier. Do you have three wives in Utah? Are you secretly a trapeze artist or something?"

"Good guys do exist, you know."

"In D.C.?" I said, laughing.

"You have a point." He looked at me askance. "Does that mean there's a catch with you?"

"Oh, there's a catch," I said, letting the mystery hang in the air like dangling carrots.

I took another sip of the old fashioned as his gaze lingered on me, the silence between us heavy with unspoken desires and uncharted territory. I couldn't deny the pull I felt toward him, a magnetic force that seemed to defy the voice in me that reminded me I was not of his kind.

As if sensing my internal struggle, he stepped closer, his hand brushing against mine on the bar. The touch sent a shiver down my spine, igniting a spark of longing within me that I tried so hard to suppress. But his gaze held mine captive, his eyes filled with a mixture of curiosity and something deeper, something that mirrored the emotions swirling inside me.

I set down my glass and stood straight, feeling a sudden urge to escape the intensity of the moment. With a playful smile, I gestured for him to follow me as I walked towards another room.

"More books," I said, noting another grand display.

"You never know when you'll need some Alexis de Tocqueville."

"Fair point," I said, scanning the shelves.

I couldn't help but marvel at the collection as I traced my fingers over the spines of the volumes, feeling the texture of history under my touch. The air was thick with anticipation, every glance exchanged between us charged with unspoken longing.

He stepped closer to point out a book, his presence enveloping me like a comforting embrace. "You'll like this one," he said, pulling out a book titled 'The Great Switch'.

As he did, I felt his body press against my side and I suddenly couldn't care less about the book. He handed me the book and I put my hand on it without grasping it, then ran my hand over his hand, then wrist, and then to his arm, clutching him with both arms and pulling him closer. I swiveled my hips so that they were square with his and he leaned against me.

"It's my favorite book ever," I let out like a gasp for air.

"You can't judge a book by its cover."

Our eyes locked, a silent agreement passing between us as

I craned my neck and pressed my lips against his. The moment our lips met, it felt like a spark ignited within me, setting my senses ablaze with desire. His touch was electric, sending waves of pleasure cascading through me as we tumbled into a dance of passion and yearning.

As we kissed fervently, our hands roamed feverishly over each other's bodies, eager and hungry for more. The air crackled with tension and desire, the heat between us palpable as we unraveled in each other's embrace. I managed to undo his tie and he slid his hand under my jacket to let that fall to the floor like forgotten inhibitions, the weight of the moment heavy with anticipation and raw need.

But, just as I thought we were finally giving in to the irresistible pull between us, he suddenly pulled away, his breath ragged and eyes filled with a mix of longing and restraint. I could see the internal struggle mirrored in his gaze, a battle between passion and principle waging within him.

"We shouldn't do this," he whispered hoarsely, his voice barely audible above the thrumming of my own heartbeats.

"What? Read books?" I searched his eyes for any sign of doubt, any hesitation that would give me an excuse to push forward, but all I found was unwavering resolve.

I let out a frustrated sigh, my body still humming with the remnants of desire as I took a step back, trying to catch my breath and steady my racing heart. The sudden halt in our fervent encounter left me feeling like a fire abruptly extinguished, the embers of passion slowly fading into a dull ache of longing.

"So conservative," I muttered under my breath, softening my

disappointment with a little teasing.

"Like, conservative, conservative!" he confirmed.

"The most conservative man I know," I said, patting him on his shirt collar. It was meant as a friendly gesture, but simply touching him made my blood surge and I couldn't help myself from caressing his neck and pulling my lips up to his again for more kisses.

With more kisses, came more touching and we found ourselves working on buttons and loosening clothes again.

But before we made much progress, he leaned back again and sighed. "We'd better cool it," he said.

"Yes," I said, then slipped my hand under his shirt to feel his chest. Good grief. His muscles were firm and powerful and I was legitimately melting. "It's so hot in here."

I could tell he was struggling as much as I was. He put his hand on my clavicle, mimicking me, and slid his hand under my blouse and bra strap. But before he got too far, he pulled his hand away and took a deep breath, again throttling my budding anticipation.

"It used to be that the woman would be the one stopping the man," I said, disillusionment dotting my playfulness.

"The great switch," he said, nodding.

Taking a step back, he smiled at me, his eyes filled with a mix of desire and respect. "Hey, you'll appreciate this," he suggested, leading me into his office, where a whole trove of campaign materials cluttered an otherwise stately decor.

I was somewhat interested to see all of his campaign stuff, the posters, the schedules, the detailed plans laid out on his desk. But it was just a slight distraction from my main focus of those pectorals and those hands of his.

"So, are you waiting for marriage or something?" I asked, curiosity lacing my tone as I tried to unravel the enigma that was William Benjamin.

His nod was firm, almost resolute, his commitment to his values shining through. "Conservative, conservative, remember?" he repeated, a mantra that seemed to zap me every time.

Ugh, of course he was. Although I respected it, I couldn't help but to think that whatever potential we had was probably gone. Of course, I fooled myself into believing that it was for the better. I was a liberal feminist after all. I didn't want to be with some misogynist pig.

"So," I continued the interrogation, "you're probably looking for a stay-at-home wife and four dozen children, aren't you?"

"Of course," he said without missing a beat. "Aren't you?"

I burst out laughing. "That's hilarious."

"Why? You said you were conservative."

"I said I was conservative, not Victorian," I shot back. "I mean, are you going to take away my voting rights next? You want me to walk behind you on the way to the bloodletting?"

He shrugged. "Sounds great."

"Oh!" I shouted, hitting him on the chest. I knew he was playing, but was he? "Any modern woman with an ounce of self-respect would storm out of here! But I can't!"

"Why not?"

"Because . . . ," I stammered, rubbing his chest again, "because . . . ," and I curved my arms around his shoulders and pulled myself up to him, "because . . . ."

He leaned in toward me as if he were about to kiss me again. "Because you know I'm right," he said.

And I slapped his chest as I turned away, letting out a hybrid huff and laugh. "You are trouble!" I asserted as I pretended to look through his campaign materials. "So, here's a thought."

"Hit me."

"Amanda said that a man won't marry a woman if she doesn't have at least two of the three big traits—looks, brains, money."

"Why not all three?"

"Ugh! Of course you would need all three." I shook my head.

He thought a little more about it. "No, a woman is complementary to a man. She should have what a man doesn't have."

"Okay," I said.

"Any man worth his salt is going to provide money, so he doesn't need her to have money. Looks and brains should do it."

"What if she only has one trait? Are you going to marry her?"

"Probably not."

"Makes sense right?"

"But Amanda forgot the fourth trait," he said.

"What's that?"

"Virtue," he said with a big grin. "And that one trumps the others."

I rolled my eyes and groaned. "You are so medieval!"

"What?! It's true," he insisted. "There's nothing more attractive than a virtuous woman."

I let out a deep breath, trying to contain the mix of frustration and amusement bubbling inside me. His old-fashioned views were like a relic from another era, and yet there was something intriguing about his unyielding stance on virtue. It was like an invisible force between us, pulling at our banter and adding a layer of tension to every word we exchanged.

As I glanced up from his campaign materials, my eyes locked with his, and for a moment, the room was charged with unspoken desires. I took a step closer as a mischievous smile tugged at my lips. "Virtue may be admirable, but it's much more fun to be unvirtuous," I said softly, my voice laced with playful defiance.

His gaze flickered with a mixture of surprise and intrigue, his features betraying a hint of uncertainty. I reached out, trailing my fingers lightly along his jawline, savoring the way his breath caught at my touch. The air between us crackled with a newfound tension, thick with unspoken desires and forbidden possibilities. His eyes darkened, a silent challenge passing between us as I leaned in closer, the scent of his cologne enveloping me in a dizzying haze.

"Not going to happen," he murmured, his voice low and husky, betraying the smoldering intensity that simmered beneath his composed demeanor.

His certainty and resolve was so deflating and at the same time so alluring. "Are you filibustering me?"

"Mmhm," he replied.

"I don't know. Amanda might be right about you," I said.

"Oh yeah, about what?"

"She said you're either a saint or a eunuch."

He burst out laughing. "Well, I'm definitely not a eunuch," he said.

I shook my head, grinning. "Prove it."

He clicked his tongue and smiled. "I think I'll have to disappoint you on that one," he teased, the corners of his mouth lifting in a playful smirk. His refusal only fueled the spark of mischief in my eyes, and I decided to push the boundaries a bit further.

Leaning in even closer, I let my breath linger tantalizingly close to his ear, feeling the warmth of his skin against mine. "This could be your only chance," I whispered, my voice laced with a seductive undertone that seemed to catch him off guard.

And then, in a flash, he turned toward the bar and left me hanging. "Want another drink?"

"Ugh!" I sighed.

* * *

I slumped on his desk, blissfully frustrated, feeling a mix of anticipation and exasperation swirling inside me. As I scanned the desk, my eyes fell on a campaign finance folder that instantly piqued my interest. My political chops started salivating at the sight of it. Flipping it open, I saw a picture that made my heart skip a beat—Barry George standing beside the extremist donor, Didier Caron. My mind raced with the implications of such a connection. I was suddenly shocked out of my trance thinking about the scandal it could bring.

Before I could dwell too much on the implications, William's voice broke through my thoughts.

"Enjoying the view?" he asked casually, holding out a crystal glass filled with amber liquid. I quickly shut the folder and turned around, trying my best to look nonchalant.

"You work for Barry George?" I inquired.

He nodded with closed eyes.

"Did I see a photo there of him with Didier Caron?"

"Probably some charity event," he explained, shrugging. "The Democrats have been trying to make a big deal of the relationship for months."

"It kind of *is* a big deal isn't it? Caron is one of the most notorious businessmen in the world."

William nodded. "But they can't make the link without the ledger, which they'll never get."

I took a sip of the drink he handed me, letting the smooth liquid distract me for a moment.

I couldn't shake off the weight of that photo burning in my mind. The implications it held were monumental, but I had to tread carefully. Revealing my true intentions could jeopardize everything, including my own position within Kenton Peats' campaign.

I couldn't hide the turmoil churning inside me as I stood there, trying to maintain a facade of casual interest. The gravity of the situation with Barry George and Didier Caron loomed over me like a dark cloud, casting shadows of doubt on every decision I made. William's nonchalant attitude only added fuel to the fire burning within me, and I knew I had to tread carefully.

As his gaze lingered on me, I took another sip of the amber liquid, the taste failing to distract me this time. The folder with the incriminating photo lay closed on his desk, a silent reminder of the dangerous game I found myself in.

"You seem lost in thought," William commented, his voice drawing me back to the present moment.

I forced a smile, my mind racing through possible scenarios and outcomes. "Just contemplating the complexities of politics," I replied vaguely, hoping to deflect any suspicion.

"Indeed."

"Well, Mr. Victorian," I said, handing him back his drink. "It's been quite a night."

"What? Leaving so soon?"

"Well, if you're a saint or a eunuch, either way, you have no use for me," I said, and tramped out to grab my jacket.

"Well, let me walk you home—do you live nearby?"

"No, please," I said, turning to face him and almost placing my hand on his chest again. "I think I've had enough chivalry for one night."

"I can fetch you an Uber."

"No, William," I said, pausing and looking down before I glanced back up at him and pulled myself up to kiss him and press my body against his as if in one last gasp of bliss. When I released him, he stood there frozen like a child. "Let me keep just a little bit of feminist pride, all right?"

He relented with a smile. "Hey, I need your number."

"What for?" I whined, only half serious.

"I don't know, book recommendations?"

"Fine!" I said, and he took down my number into his phone. "Just don't ask if I got home safely okay?"

"You don't make it easy to be a gentleman, do you?"

I gave him a long, scalding look. I could have slapped him or gave him the biggest kiss. I seriously don't know which I wanted to do more.

"What?" he said, laughing. "Okay, only business!"

"We're never going to see each other again, you know."

He grinned. "I'm not so sure about that."

And with that I swept myself out of the door in a breeze.

CHAPTER 7

THE SHRILL RING of the alarm dragged me back from the edge of sleep, and I winced, my head pounding in protest. Squinting at the harsh light of day that had infiltrated my apartment, I groped for my phone, fumbling to silence its insistent clamor. The night before was a blurry montage of political banter and one too many old fashioned cocktails, leaving me with a hangover that felt like a marching band was parading down my skull's Main Street.

Not only did I have a slight hangover from the drinks, I was also hungover from my close call with Mr. Republican himself. I don't know why it should have even mattered to me, but I felt a pang of disappointment at the way that it ended. There was definitely something there, even if it were like Romeo and Juliet and destined for mutual demise.

In a flash, I swung out of bed and into the bathroom to get ready for work, and in less than a half hour I was on my way to the office.

At the campaign, I jumped into my tasks and waited for my coffee to do its magic.

"Libby Hart, strategist extraordinaire, how do you plead in the case of last night's shenanigans?" Gabby's voice was all mischief and mirth as she swept up to my desk, her wild curls bouncing with each step.

"Guilty," I groaned, pressing a cool hand to my forehead. "But only of dancing with a bottle labeled 'Regret.'"

"Spill it, Lib. Did you and Will do the horizontal tango, or what?" Gabby's eyebrows waggled comically, and I couldn't help but snort despite the ache in my temples.

"Hardly," I replied, shaking my head. "Our boy is saving himself for marriage."

"No way! Mister Tall, Dark, and Republican is a virgin? Talk about a unicorn." Gabby's eyes were wide with disbelief, and I chuckled at the absurdity of it all.

"Right?" I said with a playful smirk. "Because nothing screams 'eligible' like a man who won't put out until you put a ring on it."

"Libby Hart, cynic of romance," Gabby teased, leaning against my desk. "But seriously, are you going to pursue Prince Charming, or what?"

I paused, considering the question. My heart raced at the thought of William—his earnest blue eyes, the way his laughter seemed to resonate in my chest. He was an enigma, wrapped in conservative values, inside a navy blue suit. But pursuing him?

"Gabby, he's like a walking, talking political ad for 'Family Values,'" I said, my voice tinged with skepticism. "Could you see me, Libby 'Liberated' Hart, cozying up to someone who probably has a bumper sticker that says 'Wait for the Mate'?"

"Girl, he might be worth it."

I let the image of his buff chest fill my mind. "He might be."

"Are you sure you didn't get it on, girl?" she asked. "I've seen that look before."

"We didn't. But he did take me to his apartment and we made out in his library."

"Oh, now it's on!"

"No, it's not going to work."

"It doesn't sound that way to me."

"Besides, he probably wouldn't go for me if he knew I were a Democrat."

"What?! You didn't tell him?"

"He actually thinks I'm a conservative Republican."

"Oh my goodness, child," she said breathlessly. "That is too funny."

"No, I don't think I'm the future Missus Benjamin." I was being silly, but the melancholy was unmistakable.

"Love in the time of campaign season," Gabby quipped, her grin infectious. "Just don't let Vanessa catch you daydreaming, or she'll have you drafting policy proposals on your first date."

"Or worse, she'll volunteer us for a get-out-the-vote campaign," I added dryly, eliciting a burst of laughter from both of us.

"God forbid," Gabby said, wiping away a tear. "All right, work awaits us, my brain-strained friend. Let's go make some political magic—or at least try not to vomit on any potential voters."

I nodded, standing up a little too quickly and regretting it immediately. With a steadying breath, I straightened my blazer and prepared to face the day, the image of William Benjamin lingering in my mind like the ghost of William Henry Harrison.

* * *

The sun was barely up, and the campaign office already felt like a pressure cooker ready to explode. I was nursing my third coffee when Vanessa Martinez swept into the room like a storm in stilettos, her expression alone furious enough to make interns scatter.

Malcolm was trying to explain to her the work I had done the previous day, but she wasn't having any of it. "It's tepid. We need fire, not a lukewarm bath. We need it done again."

My stomach sank. I'd thought the work I had done was some of my best—punchy, concise, just shy of slanderous.

"Yes, Vanessa," Malcolm said like a scorned puppy.

Beside me, Gabby leaned in, her wild curls a halo in the fluorescent light. "Don't sweat it," she murmured, "Vanessa's standards are like mythical creatures—rumored to exist but never actually seen."

"Thanks, Gabs," I whispered back, allowing myself a half-smile.

"Meeting, five minutes!" Vanessa barked across the office before disappearing as quickly as she appeared, leaving a trail of anxious whispers in her wake.

"Come on," Gabby said, nudging me toward the conference room. "Let's see what fresh hell awaits."

We filed in with the rest of the staff, standing shoulder-to-shoulder around a whiteboard littered with graphs and numbers all trending in the wrong direction. Vanessa stood at the front, laser pointer in hand, stabbing at the board like it had personally offended her.

"Poll numbers are sagging," she announced, her tone sharp enough to slice through the tension. "We need an edge, something juicy. And I think I've found our angle." She clicked to a slide showing two men shaking hands—a photo I recognized from William's place.

"Barry George and Didier Caron," she said, the names heavy with implication. "A match made in backroom deal heaven."

"Oh my God," I whispered.

Gabby looked at me, curious. "What is it?"

"We're pretty sure that Caron is funding the campaign, but we don't know how," Vanessa growled. "George has denied it of course as he's denied that they're even friends."

Gabby watched my reaction. I turned to her, keeping my eyes ahead. "I saw this at William's place last night." Gabby gasped.

Vanessa paced like a caged animal, her heels clicking a staccato rhythm against the hardwood floor. "We need intel from the inside," she asserted, eyes scanning the room for a volunteer— or a victim. "Does anyone here know William Benjamin?"

The question hung heavy in the air, a hot potato no one dared catch. I felt Gabby's expectant gaze on me, but I ducked my head, hoping to blend into the sign-lined walls.

"Come on, Libby," Gabby whispered with a nudge.

"Shh, not so loud." I shot her a glare.

"Lib-by!" she was whispering but with as much intensity as she could muster for that decibel level.

"I don't know him."

"You made out with him in his library," Gabby insisted, her

voice a conspiratorial murmur.

"Gabby!"

"Ladies?" Vanessa screeched. "Is there something you want to share with us?"

I sat there, eyes wide and frozen. She locked eyes with me, and I could swear she saw right through my poker face. "There's a bonus in it for whoever steps up."

"Libby knows him!" Gabby blurted out before I could clamp a hand over her mouth. The room erupted in murmurs as everyone looked at me.

"Hart?" Vanessa's eyebrow arched in challenge.

I hesitated, caught between a rock and a potential career boost. My stomach churned at the thought of using Mr. Tall, Dark, and Republican for political gain. But, then again, wasn't this the game we all played in Washington?

"It's not like that," I tried.

"What is it like?"

"Um," I said, trying to buy time. "I can explain."

Vanessa was clearly intrigued, but she stepped to the side as if to transition away from the topic. "After this meeting," she said, "in my office."

I could do nothing but nod. And when Vanessa continued onto the next topic, I turned to Gabby with beady eyes. "Thanks a lot!"

Gabby just smiled confidently and sat back in her chair.

CHAPTER 8

THE MOMENT GABBY and I stepped into Vanessa's stainless steel fortress of an office, I could feel the expectancy crackling in the air like static. She sat behind her desk, a raven among doves, her fingertips drumming a silent and impatient rhythm on the glass surface. I was surprised to see two men in black suits standing behind her desk, apparently waiting for us.

"Okay, go," Vanessa demanded without preamble, her gaze sharp enough to slice through the nervous energy we carried with us.

"Go?" I questioned, my voice trailing off as I peered over to the two men in suits.

"Don't worry, they're with the legal team."

I suddenly felt as if I were about to be arrested.

Gabby, always less inhibited, jumped in, her curly hair bouncing as she recounted the tale as if it were the juiciest piece of gossip rather than the fuse to a potential career bomb. "We were at Clifton's for happy hour and we—"

"Who's 'We'?" Vanessa interrupted.

"Libby, myself, and my friend Amanda."

"You were drinking?" Vanessa interrogated.

"Well," Gabby said, glancing at me and then back to Vanessa, "yeah. It's happy hour."

"Okay, continue."

"So, we were checking out the crowd and we spotted Mister Benjamin off to the side with a few others," Gabby recited.

"Did you know who he was?"

"Yes, we'd seen him in interviews," Gabby said.

"Go on."

"So, my friend Amanda is a little more . . . extraverted than most, and she goes to introduce herself to Benjamin."

"Why?"

"What do you mean, 'Why'?"

"Why did she go up to him?" Vanessa pressed.

Gabby was perplexed as to why it was even in question. "He's hot," she said, matter-of-factly. "She wanted to get to know him."

"Get to know him?"

"Sure, you know," Gabby said, "Biblically."

Vanessa hissed at the euphemism and one of the men cleared his throat. "Go on," Vanessa said.

"Well, Benjamin wasn't having none of that, so Amanda came back to the bar."

"He didn't go for her?"

"She struck out," Gabby said. "So Amanda and I go to the ladies room and come back and none other than William Benjamin is talking to Libby here."

Vanessa turned to me. "How'd this happen?"

I looked at Vanessa suspiciously, then up to the two men in

suits. "I was sitting there and he just sat down next to me," I said.

Vanessa started working out something in her head. "Interesting. So what happened?"

"We chatted a bit," I said.

"About what?"

"I don't remember," I said. "Something about D.C. since I'm new."

"Okay, go on."

"Oh, well, he asked me what party I was affiliated with and I said 'Republican'."

"Why did you say that?"

"Because . . . ," I said, rolling my head around, trying to come up with a reason. "He made it seem as though he wouldn't want to talk with me otherwise."

"You wanted to talk with him?"

"Well, yeah," I said, "he's hot."

"That's what I've heard."

"Anyway, we chatted a bit, and, then, after Gabby and Amanda got back, I suggested Will and I take a walk on the Mall."

"And you did?"

"We did," I said, beginning to slow down the narrative as I didn't want to reveal it all. "And we stopped by his apartment."

"You actually entered the residence?"

"Um, yeah, we had a drink."

"In his apartment, did you see campaign materials and files?"

"Yeeesss . . . ," I let out.

"Were you able to investigate them?"

"I was there as an acquaintance, not an oversight committee," I said with eyes squinted.

"That's fine," Vanessa said, oblivious. "Okay, did you do anything else?"

"No. We talked a while, and then I went home."

"Nothing else? You didn't get intimate with him?"

"I really don't think it's necessary to divulge—"

"Look, Libby, it is of the essence that we have the full picture of what went on so that we can advise the matter best."

"Advise?"

"William Benjamin is the chief of staff for the George campaign," she said. "He is one of the key figures in a very close race, and we need to take advantage of every possible strategic advantage that we can find."

I looked down as if to make sense of the mess that I had gotten myself into.

"Now," she continued, "did you sleep with him?"

I huffed in indignation.

"Libby?" Vanessa demanded.

"No," I said.

"Okay," she said, a series of thoughts rushing through her head. "Did it seem as though he was attracted to you?"

Again I huffed out a response. "How could I know?"

"You were in his apartment, weren't you?" she said. "Did he make advances? Did he try to kiss you?"

I shook my head, wondering how it had come to this. "He is a very principled man," I reported. "A gentleman. And . . . ."

"And?"

"And I am no lady."

Vanessa raised an eyebrow as she stood to walk around and think. "I think it can work," she said to one of the men, who shrugged. "Okay, here's what we have to do."

I held my breath for my sentencing. Vanessa's eyes narrowed, the look on her face one I'd seen too many times: the cogs turning, the strategist plotting.

"Libby." It wasn't a question, but a command. Her voice dropped to a conspiratorial whisper. "You're going to date him."

"Date him?" My voice pitched high enough to rival the squeak of the leather chair I sat in.

"Yes," Vanessa said, still shuffling through thoughts in her head. "Do you have plans to see him again?"

"No," I said, exasperated. "That was it."

"Do you have his contact information?"

"Yes. We exchanged numbers."

"Okay, good," she said. "So, you'll text him or get into touch with him, or whatever it is that you do, and go out with him."

"Wha—what if he isn't interested?" I said, a hypothetical that could very well have been the case.

"You have to ensure that he is interested," she said, cold as a corpse.

"I'm pretty sure that he has a mind of his own and I can't make him want to date me."

"Eh," she said, "don't sell yourself short. You're a very attractive woman, and all the signs indicate that he's attracted to you."

Well I didn't want to deny that.

"Sure," she said, "get in touch with him, and go out a few times, do what you need to do to get close enough that he trusts you with his files."

"And then?"

"And then you'll obtain the ledger," she said, easing through her words so as to not offend the suits.

"That's not remotely legal, is it?"

"It is," she said, "as long as you get him to give you the files."

"Why would he do that?"

"Because . . . ," she said, leaning back with an air of utter superiority, "you're a Republican. This is paramount—it is essential that he continue to believe that you're a Republican on his side."

I shook my head in disbelief. "Look, I don't know how things are done around here, but where I'm from, we don't get into romantic relationships in order to incriminate our political enemies."

"Libby, look," Vanessa said, posting her hands on her desk as if it were a lectern, "I'm sure that even where you're from you know how corrupt Barry George is. He's pompous, conniving, greedy, sexist, homophobic, xenophobic, transphobic, arachnophobic, you name it, he has a phobia about it. And this is all besides the policies the man is pushing. He's destroying our democracy. Why the voters put him in office is beyond me. But what we do know is that he's lying to them. To us. To everyone. And we have a duty to uncover the truth. And this is one way that could mean the difference between that man getting re-elected and a good and noble challenger to take his place."

She spoke as if she were on the campaign trail. And, do you know what? It worked. I was riled up. I agreed with everything she was saying, and I knew she was right.

"Now, we need you to do this," she continued. "We'll provide you with everything you need to make it believable—money, resources, a new apartment if you'd like, everything. All we need is for you to say 'Yes'."

I have to admit, it did sound like an amazing offer. "I just . . . ."

"Yes?"

"I just didn't realize that when I came to D.C. I would be coming to be a spy."

"You don't have to put it that way," Vanessa assured me. "Think of it more as an investigative reporter."

"Okay . . . ," I said, scanning the floor for an answer. "It's still lying, isn't it?"

Vanessa took in a big breath through her nose. "To be frank," she said, "yes, it is. But listen. If you can stop this man from getting re-elected, even if you have to fib a little, then I think you'd agree that it's worth it."

I nodded solemnly.

"Libby," she said, "sometimes we have to do a lesser evil to accomplish the greater good. That's what politics is all about."

I sighed, knowing that she was right, but wishing that she didn't have to be.

"I have to think about it," I said.

"You can have the rest of the day off if you'd like," she said. "In fact, it's probably best that you're not seen here at headquarters from here on. Just send me a text one way or another."

"Okay."

"If you want to talk it over with Gabby, feel free. But, no one else outside of the people in this room knows about this. Okay?"

I agreed, and Gabby and I stood up to leave.

CHAPTER 9

I SLID INTO the plush booth of Chez Amour, a cozy nook that smelled like garlic and promises. Gabby, already sipping on something pink and fizzy, beamed at me from across the table with those eyes that could sell ice to Eskimos.

"Okay, so, is this really happening?" she asked, her wild curls bouncing as she leaned in. "A loft overlooking the Potomac, a shiny new Beamer, and a fancy job at a tech company. You're kind of a big deal, Libs."

My heart raced at the thrill of it all, but my palms were slick with a cold sweat. I picked up the wine menu, if only to have something to do with my hands. "It's a lot," I confessed, my voice a notch higher than usual. "I mean, sure, what political strategist wouldn't want to be a . . . ."

"Spy?" Gabby finished, her smile wicked. She plucked the menu from my grip and signaled the waiter for a bottle of the house white. "You're going in deep cover, babe. It's straight out of a movie."

"Right. A movie where the protagonist has a mental breakdown," I countered, forcing a laugh that didn't quite reach my eyes.

"No way," Gabby reassured, "you've got this. Just remember what Vanessa said about Barry George—these guys are bad dudes, and anything you can do to help beat them will be for the greater good."

"I know," I said, still not convinced. "It just feels like cheating somehow. I don't want to hurt anyone."

"Well, they shouldn't be working for the bad guys, then."

"Good point," I said, but I didn't believe it.

"Libby Hart, since when did you become such a scaredy-cat?" Gabby chided, her eyes dancing with mischief. "You've faced down senators and spin doctors. You can handle one handsome policy wonk."

I smiled in response, but I was definitely a scaredy-cat.

"Listen, all's fair in love and politics, you know," she said. "In D.C., if you lose that killer instinct, you're dead."

She was right. That was politics for you. And that was the line of work I was in. It was my choice in the end.

"And besides," she said, "if you're going to spy on somebody, I can think of a few who would be less appealing than William Benjamin." Gabby waggled her eyebrows suggestively. "He is serious eye candy, Libs. And he's smart, charming, and. . . . "

"Yeah," I said, sighing, and took another look at the menu as the waiter brought our drinks, the sound mingling with the soft strains of jazz in the background. As I looked into Gabby's earnest face, the craziness of it all seemed almost . . . exciting.

I took a sip of wine, the cool liquid emboldening me just a touch.

"You know what's really terrifying?" I started, feeling the weight of the fork in my hand like the gravity of my confession. "It's not just the lying or the espionage—it's William."

"William?" Gabby propped her chin on her hand, the candle-light flickering playfully across her curious gaze.

"Yep." I set down my wine with more of a thud than intended. "The guy is . . . well, he's something else. And that's the problem. If I spend too much time with him, I fear I might just . . . ."

"Fall head over heels for him?" Gabby interjected with a smirk.

"Exactly," I sighed, staring into my wine glass as if it held all the answers. "How can I fight against everything he stands for if I'm busy swooning every time he talks about tax reforms?"

"It's a distinct possibility."

"What if Mr. Right-wing is actually Mr. Right?"

"Libby, love," Gabby said, reaching across the table to give my hand a reassuring squeeze, "who says you can't have a little fun while saving the world?"

"Yeah, but what kind of yo-yo falls in love with the guy she's trying to destroy?" I retorted, but her infectious optimism was already gnawing at my resolve.

"I don't think you can worry about that," she said. "Just one step at a time."

"Right. So what's the first step?"

"You need to decide soon. The clock's ticking, and we need to get you in touch with William before he thinks you've ghosted him."

"About that . . . ," I trailed off, recalling the notification that had popped up on my phone earlier. "He's already texted me."

"Really?" Her eyebrows shot up. "When?"

"This morning."

"WTF? This guy is not even messing around."

"I'm sure it was just the typical starter text after a night of kissing."

"Oh yeah?" Gabby said, intrigued. "What did he say?"

"Your guess is as good as mine," I admitted, pulling out my phone but leaving it face-down on the table. "I haven't read it. I was trying to delay the inevitable reply."

"Libby Hart!" Gabby exclaimed, half amused, half exasperated. "You are sitting on a goldmine, and you're treating it like a jury duty summons!"

"Fine, fine." I surrendered, flipping the phone over and tapping the screen. My heart did an involuntary somersault as his name lit up my notifications. With a deep breath that did nothing to steady my nerves, I opened the message.

My thumb hovered over the screen, the glow of the message casting a pale light on our expectant faces. "Listen to this," I said, clearing my throat for dramatic effect. "'I really enjoyed our filibuster last night. Hoping you got back safe and sound.'"

"Oh, he's a nerd," Gabby cooed with a grin.

"Seriously," I murmured, a smile tugging at the corner of my lips despite the anxiety knotting my stomach.

"Come on, hit him back with something that'll make his convention convene," Gabby urged, wiggling her eyebrows playfully.

I chewed my lip, fingers dancing across the keyboard before settling on a response. "All right, here goes nothing." I typed quickly, feeling a mix of trepidation and thrill. "'You said only business, sir. I enjoyed the filibuster too.'"

"Send it! Send it!" Gabby bounced in her seat as I pressed the button, dispatching my flirty retort into the political wilderness of our budding relationship.

We turned back to our plates, our laughter mingling with the low hum of the restaurant. I skewered a cherry tomato with my fork, watching it burst—a metaphorical pop to my bubble of denial. I didn't really believe Will would be deterred from his busy work day to bother with me.

But, wouldn't you know it, before I could savor the tangy sweetness, my phone buzzed insistently against the table linens.

"Speak of the devil," I muttered, picking up my device. There it was—a message punctuated with wit and a hint of challenge. "He says, 'Apologies. Madame President, I rise to inquire about the well-being and safe arrival of my esteemed colleague after last night's proceedings.'"

"Oh God, he's totally into you," Gabby squealed.

"Or he's just very dedicated to his job," I countered, skepticism shading my voice.

"Stop playing defense, girl, and start playing to win," Gabby pressed.

"Fine. I hope this doesn't end in gridlock." I quickly composed another message: "'The Senator's concern for the Speaker's well-being is duly noted and appreciated. I can confirm that the Speaker arrived home safely and without incident.'"

"If anyone can match his nerdiness, it's you," Gabby teased.

We returned to our meals, but he replied too quickly to get

far.

I glanced down at my phone and laughed. "'I'm glad to hear that, Madame President. Your safety is of paramount concern to this Assembly.'"

"I'll say," Gabby said.

"'Thank you, Senator. Your concern warms the cockles of my heart.'"

I looked at Gabby for guidance.

"Oh this is much better than Netflix," she said.

I sent it and waited for a reply. Which came within minutes.

"'I rise to introduce Senate Bill 123, also known as National Mall Run Act.'" I looked up to Gabby.

"I think he's asking you on a date," she said.

"What comes next, in Parliamentary Procedure?"

"Oh, he needs to explain the bill," she said. "You have to give him the floor."

"'The Senator from Washington D.C. has the floor to discuss the purpose and provisions of the bill.'" I squealed as I hit send.

"'Thank you Madame President. Senate Bill 123 allocates federal funds for the rehabilitation of a fantastic conversation between the Senator from Washington D.C. and the Assembly's President. Additionally, the bill establishes grant programs to support physical fitness in the form of running the National Mall at 11 a.m.'"

"Going for a run as a first date?" Gabby posed, shrugging.

I was grinning uncontrollably as I typed a reply. "'Senator, the Bill has been introduced and referred to the appropriate committee. Is there further business in this matter?'"

Gabby shook her head. "Uhumm, girl. He don't know what he's getting with you."

"'Madame President, I move to pass the Bill with unanimous consent.'"

"'Do I have a second?'"

"'Martin Van Buren's chandelier seconds the motion.'"

I laughed and looked at Gabby. "Don't ask."

"'Senate Bill 123, also known as the National Mall Run Act has been moved and seconded. All those in favor say Aye.'"

"'Aye.'"

"'The Ayes have it. The motion is adopted. The National Mall Run Act is hereby scheduled.'"

I put my phone down and glanced at Gabby with a mix of excitement and worry. "I guess I'm going out with Mr. Right-wing."

"This is gon be good!" she said with a mischievous giggle.

* * *

I folded a stack of laundry with less precision than I'd allocate to campaign leaflets, my brain far from the mundane task. The phone, that pocket-sized Pandora's box, lay on the kitchen counter, its screen casting a soft glow in the dim light of my apartment. Every few minutes, it buzzed with William's responses, and I found myself tiptoeing a precarious line between professional duty and personal intrigue.

"Spying on the enemy is one thing," I muttered to myself as I paired socks, "falling for him is like . . . fraternizing with the foe."

And yet, there was something about him—something disarmingly genuine. I shot back a playful text, my fingertips hesitating just a moment before pressing send. "Is this how Mata Hari felt? Or am I just channeling high school crush anxiety?"

I could almost hear Gabby's voice in my head, egging me on with her devil-may-care attitude. "Libby Hart doesn't do anything halfway," she'd say, pushing me towards the edge of reason. "Go big or go home."

"Going home" wasn't an option. I felt like I was already there. And going "big" had taken on a whole new meaning. As I made my way to the bedroom, shedding the day's attire for my pajamas, I reviewed William's texts and imagined him saying them to me with that smooth voice and those smiling eyes.

I held the phone to my chest as if I could imitate the feeling of an embrace. It was ridiculous, but it sufficed. There was just one last thing that I had to do before going to bed and waking up as a spy.

My thumb hovered over Vanessa's contact before tapping out a message with equal parts trepidation and resolve.

'I'm in.'

Short, unequivocal, like the final gavel strike in a floor debate.

'Good,' Vanessa's reply came back, as swift and sharp as her trademark stilettos. 'Baxter will be in touch with your personal effects.'

"Personal effects," I hummed, setting the phone down and flicking off the lights. In the darkness, the contours of my room blurred, and so did the lines of my new mission. With every beat of my heart against the cool screen of the phone, the stakes grew higher, and so did the thrill. Sleep would come eventually, but dreams of running dates and covert operations would keep my mind churning.

CHAPTER 10

I JOLTED AWAKE to the staccato rhythm of a firm knock. Rubbing sleep from my eyes, I stumbled toward the door, fumbling with the chain lock before swinging it open. There stood Baxter, as if he'd waltzed off the pages of a legal thriller—pristine black suit, not a wrinkle in sight, briefcase in hand like a shield of professionalism.

"Good morning, Miss Hart," he said, his voice carrying the no-nonsense timbre I remembered from that shark tank meeting with Vanessa. "I trust you slept well."

"Like a baby, if the baby was anticipating a covert operation," I blabbed, my heart kick-drumming against my ribs. Waking up to Baxter was more jarring than an espresso.

"Ah," he responded, a twinkle of amusement in his eyes that didn't reach his lips. "Well, then, let's get to it."

With a precision that would make a Swiss watch jealous, he handed me a set of keys that gleamed under the harsh light of my entryway and a folder thick enough to double as a weapon.

"Here are the keys to your new apartment, vehicle, and the details of your faux employment," Baxter explained, stepping aside to allow me space to process it all. "Now, the job is at a real tech company here in D.C., and you don't have to go to the office, but it will help if you know a good deal about them in case it comes up in conversation."

"You guys have thought of everything," I muttered, taking the proffered items with hands that betrayed a slight tremor. My fingers brushed against his cool ones, and I couldn't help but notice the contrast between his icy composure and my own nervous energy.

"Your eagerness is palpable, Miss Hart," Baxter observed, one eyebrow arching ever so slightly.

"Call it what you will, Mister Baxter. I call it caffeine deficiency." I cracked a smile, trying to mask the whirlwind of anticipation swirling inside me.

As I flipped through the folder, each page revealed a new layer of my impending life. A stunning condo in the heart of Georgetown, a sleek car that probably had more horsepower than I knew what to do with, and a cover job that sounded so convincing I almost believed it myself.

"Wow, you guys really outdid yourselves with the details," I remarked, whistling lowly as my gaze darted across the print. "I was expecting a secret handshake or a decoder ring."

"Alas, Miss Hart, we can't afford everything," he deadpanned, though the corner of his mouth twitched in a semblance of a suppressed smile.

"Shame."

"Indeed. If there's nothing else, I'll leave you to acclimate to your new . . . accessories." Baxter's voice was smooth, the kind of tone that could calm a storm or argue a case with equal ease.

"Wait, Baxter!" The words tumbled out before I could stop them. "I mean—thank you. This is all a bit overwhelming, but I appreciate the . . . thoroughness."

"Merely doing my job," he replied, a flicker of warmth in his otherwise stoic expression. "Remember, discretion is paramount, Miss Hart. Your role in this campaign is critical."

"Understood. I'll be as silent as a mime . . . with a vow of silence."

"Very poetic," Baxter acknowledged with a nod, then turned on his heel, departing with the same efficiency he arrived with.

Closing the door behind him, I leaned against it, letting out a breath of nervous energy. My heart raced like a candidate's on election night. Alone with my thoughts, I clutched the keys, the metallic coolness grounding me.

"Okay, Libby," I murmured to myself, summoning courage like I was gearing up for a debate. "Time to step into the unknown. Again."

The keys jangled cheerfully as I tossed them up and caught them, their sound punctuating my newfound resolve. With a folder full of secrets under my arm and a future paved with political intrigue ahead, I knew one thing for sure: life was about to get a whole lot more interesting.

* * *

I strode out of my apartment, the folder under one arm and the keys a cool, promising weight in my palm. The parking garage was dimly lit, echoing with the soft hum of city life that permeated even this concrete cavern. My heels clicked rhythmically against the asphalt, a determined drumbeat matching the quickening pulse of anticipation within me.

There it was, lurking in the shadows like a panther poised for the hunt—a glossy BMW that promised a ride as smooth as a seasoned politician's speech. I approached, admiring its sleek lines, and with a satisfying beep, unlocked it. Slipping into the driver's seat felt like sliding into a new persona—one where control and luxury were mine for the taking.

The engine purred to life, a low rumble that vibrated through the chassis and into my very core. A thrill zipped through me as I navigated the car up the ramp and into the light of day. Washington, D.C. buzzed around me, alive with the kind of electric current only found in the nation's political heartbeat. As I merged into traffic, I felt an affinity with the city—an unspoken understanding that we both thrived on power, strategy, and the occasional high-speed chase.

Monuments of history flanked me, their stoic marble and granite faces watching as I whipped by. The Capitol dome gleamed in the distance like a beacon, reminding me that I was playing in the big leagues now. I grinned at the reflection of the Washington Monument in the rear-view mirror, thinking how politics and obelisks both tended to be phallic contests of who could reach higher. Could I really compete?

Pulling up to the gates of my new condo complex, I punched in the code with an air of someone who'd been doing this all her life. The gate slid open, granting me access to a world I'd only ever glimpsed from the outside. My heart danced a jitterbug as I parked and made my way inside.

"Hello, prime time," I announced to nobody in particular, pushing open the door to my condo. The grandeur that met me stopped me dead in my tracks. The picture window framed the Potomac River like a living work of art, the water shimmering under the sun's flirtatious winks.

"Is this real life, or is this just fantasy?" I sang aloud, tossing my keys onto the counter with a clatter.

I walked into the bedroom to see an impressive king sized bed and a closet with a few choice skirt suits hanging on the rack.

Spreading my arms wide, I surrendered to gravity and fell backward onto the bed. The mattress hugged me back, whispering tales of comfort and conspiracy.

"Libby Hart," I breathed, "you've officially arrived."

But the universe has a funny way of reminding us that time waits for no one—not even for a newly minted major player with a view of the Potomac. A glance at the clock catapulted me from my reverie; I had a running date with William Benjamin and not a minute to spare.

"Show time," I said, springing up from the bed with the agility of a campaign dodging a scandal. "Let's brew this plot."

CHAPTER 11

I PULLED INTO the lot behind the Lincoln Memorial, the purr of my BMW's engine turning heads as I found a spot and hopped out. I stepped out of the vehicle like a movie star, despite the fact that I had never been one for flashiness and was a nervous wreck beyond the facade.

"Elizabeth Hart," William called out, his voice carrying over the buzz of the nearby tourists, "you're quite the vision in steel and chrome!"

"William Benjamin," I replied, sauntering over with the best casual grace I could muster. "You flatter me, and my car."

"Looks, brains, *and* money," he said, eyes twinkling as he took in my approach. "Amanda was wrong—they do exist."

"Are you calling me a unicorn?" I said. He had his hand extended, so I shook it, but then I realized that I was already going for a hug, so I ended up hugging his arm. What a dork.

"I guess you don't need a man after all," he chimed and continued stretching.

"Ha!" I laughed, joining him for a little stretch. "For some things, yes."

"So, I had you pegged as a campaign strategist, given your policy knowledge," he said, eyeing me through squints. "But now I'm leaning toward consultant or, maybe even lawyer."

"Would you believe, tech company?" I thought I played it off pretty well, but then he rolled his head around as if to make sense of it.

"Maybe," he said. "Is it here in the District?"

"Oh, no, it's . . . a small firm . . . over in Arlington."

"Polaris?" he shot back, eager.

I was a deer in headlights. "Yes, how did you . . . ?"

"I've got a good friend who works over there."

"You don't say," I said, suddenly mortified.

"James Richards, he's over in accounting."

I shook my head.

"No?" he pressed.

"No, we try not to interact with the accounting folks over in marketing," I tried.

"Oh, how about Shontelle Warren? She's in marketing."

"Good grief, do you know everyone?" I jested.

"It does come with the territory."

"True," I said. "I'll keep an eye out for her."

"Well, I'm sure your talents are put to good use there, but I can't imagine someone like you not calling the shots on outreach or coming up with new policy suggestions."

"I get a fair share of politics at my company," I said. "But, yes, I do enjoy the strategy behind it all."

"We politicos are a different breed."

"That's for sure."

"It's almost like we're not living if we're not solving the world's problems before breakfast."

"So," I said, "I'm just going to have to live vicariously through you."

"I'll do my best to keep you engaged."

"I have every confidence that you will," I said, glancing over toward the Mall.

"I figured we would head up to the Capitol and back," he said. "It's about five miles round trip."

"Oh, just a leisurely stroll," I teased.

"I mean, we could go to the Washington Monument and back if the Capitol's too far."

"Oh no, not too far at all," I said, my competitiveness getting the best of me.

"I'll let you set the pace," he said.

"Try and keep up," I returned, and took off running at a brisk clip.

He caught up in no time and we rounded the Memorial to head onto the Mall at a fierce pace.

"So, what's the most exciting thing you're working on for the campaign?" I inquired.

"Oh, I'm really excited about Barry's flat tax idea," he said, getting visibly animated just introducing it. "We've worked it out so that it brings in more revenue than the current system."

"Isn't a flat tax regressive, though?" I said, unable to resist punching holes in the idea.

"That's what the Democrats say," he said, and I cleared my throat. "But when you look at the data, it begins to look a lot fairer for all."

"Everyone pays the same amount, right?"

"Everyone pays the same *rate*," he said, "but everyone pays a different *amount* based on their income." As he explained it, he became downright jovial as he ran, a huge smile stretched across his face, and hands and arms flailing about as if to illustrate. I couldn't help but to appreciate his zeal, even if I still didn't buy the policy idea.

"The real benefit comes with the plan's simplicity," he said. "There are so many deductions and loopholes in the current system that only the wealthy can take advantage of that they end up paying a much smaller amount than the rest of us."

He paused and pointed back to my BMW. "Well, you might be in that top one percent," he said, making me laugh, "so you might not find this so appealing."

"No, I totally get it," I said with a smirk.

We rounded the Washington Monument and continued down toward the Capitol, my energy strangely increasing even as we continued to pick up the pace.

"The reduction of burden on the middle class, that's really where we win," he said. His eyes shone with a fervor I couldn't help but admire, even as my mind screamed in opposition.

"Interesting," I interjected, suppressing the urge to debate him point for point.

"I just realized something," he said, turning slightly as if to focus. "Most of the time I'm talking about this, it's with people who are trying to undercut my argument with logical fallacies. It's nice to have these discussions without someone trying to bite my head off."

My eyes bulged out of their sockets, but I laughed it off. "Always better to discuss than argue," I returned smoothly.

"Exactly! If everyone in politics thought like you . . . ," he trailed off, shaking his head as if marveling at the impossibility.

"Who knows?" I posed, batting my lashes with mock innocence. "Maybe one day they will."

"Maybe they will," he echoed, smiling at me with something like admiration—or was it challenge? Either way, I was ready. After all, isn't politics just another stage, and all of us merely players?

"Will!" The sudden intrusion shattered our bubble. A pudgy young man in a disheveled suit and tie askew, appeared running down the path behind us like a storm cloud chasing after us. "You haven't answered my texts—I've been trying to contact you."

We slowed our pace and came to a stop to meet up with him.

"I'm on my lunch break," he explained with a calmness that seemed almost unnatural for a man who had just been running an eight-minute mile.

"Oh," the man said, panting from his short trot.

"Elizabeth Hart, this is Simon Katz, my chief strategist."

"Glad to meet you," I said, waving to avoid a sweaty handshake.

"Will, I need to talk with you . . . in private," he said, glancing at me.

"Is now the best time?" William asked.

"It can't wait."

"Well, go ahead and tell me, then."

"I'd rather not . . . ," Simon said.

"Don't worry," William assured. "She's one of us, Simon. Anything you have to say can be said in front of her."

Simon's eyes narrowed as if to scrutinize me, his gaze sharp enough to slice through my slim veneer. "But this is important."

"Better tell me quick, then," William said.

"All right," Simon began, lowering his voice to a whisper that still managed to cut through the noise of the bustling city street. "I may have a breakthrough on our campaign financing issue."

I tried not to act interested, but it sounded a lot like they were talking about our old buddy Didier Caron.

"Financing issue?" William's eyebrow arched, and I could see the gears turning behind those intent blue eyes.

"Yes, the one having to do with a particular donor," Simon hissed, his excitement palpable.

"Yes, I know the one," William murmured, and then glanced at me. "What's going on?"

"The folks over at Liberty—" Simon said, cutting himself off to look at me again. "The action committee have agreed to the deal."

"Oh," William said, actually surprised. "That's great news."

"Yeah," Simon said, "and everything should be in place by the InterContinental event."

Will pumped his fist, thinking about the implications. "Awesome work, Simon."

"They just need you to give the green light," he said.

"Okay," William said. "I'll be back at the office at one."

"They really want to move on this now," Simon said while

gnashing his teeth.

"They can wait an hour," William said, patting down the air.

"But, if . . . ," Simon said, looked at me and then moaned. "Okay, but hurry."

William nodded and Simon scampered off of the path and down the street.

"That's Simon Katz," William said again, obviously amused.

"He seems . . . determined," I said, with a slight chuckle.

"Oh, he's determined," William said, leaning in and turning back in the direction we had been running.

"It sounds like you've got an urgent matter you've got to attend to."

"Yeah, but it can wait," he said, not convinced. "Shall we resume?"

We started running again and quickly got back into our groove, passing the front of the Capitol and turning around to the other side of the Mall.

When we got back to the parking lot, I was completely spent. I was supposedly setting the pace, but my competitive spirit and desire to impress my running mate made me keep ratcheting up the speed. William appeared exhausted too, so at least my pride wasn't hurt too much.

"Hey, so, you want a better taste of D.C. politics?" he chirped.

"Um, sure," I said, bounding my eyes back and forth.

"You should come by the office some time and see how a campaign operates," he said with a flick of his head.

"Is that . . . legal?"

He laughed. "I should hope so. We're not doing anything illegal there, so, yeah."

I raised my eyebrow thinking I'd be the judge of that. But it did seem like a golden opportunity to get the inside story and potentially get a look at that ledger. "Okay," I said, and we made plans for me to visit.

After a few stretches, we walked to our cars and I held my hand out as if for a shake. He actually picked it up and kissed it. I practically fell over. But I held it together enough to say goodbye and slink into my car.

CHAPTER 12

AS I WALKED up the stairs to my new condo, a surge of excitement bubbled up from my toes. Was this fancy Georgetown townhouse really mine? I had quite a little set up—my own space, my political boudoir, my war room adorned with stylish decor and the scent of possibility.

"Hello, beautiful," I cooed to nobody in particular, flinging my keys onto the shiny countertop. My heels clacked across the polished floor as I made a beeline for the wardrobe. Every door I swung open revealed another tier of sartorial heaven: business suits sharp enough to cut through party lines, blouses that screamed 'I have a plan for that,' and accessories that could outshine any debate stage bling.

"Okay, Libby Hart, let's see if we can't turn this strategist into a stylist." I plucked a navy blue power suit from its hanger and slipped it on. The fabric hugged my body like a promise of victory, each seam whispering sweet policy dreams. I struck a pose in the mirror, a hand on one hip, and winked at my reflection. "Madame President? Too soon?"

My chuckle echoed off the walls, filling the empty condo with the sound of my own ambition. I strolled over to the kitchen and surveyed the bar area, stocked with a row of high-end bottles with labels that suggested they'd been aged longer than some voter registrations.

"Old enough to run for president, huh?" I said, picking up a bottle of scotch with an apparent oak finish.

My phone vibrated against the cool granite countertop, yanking me from my mixology musings. Gabby's texts were a string of emojis that translated to 'gossip, champagne, and dancing'. I could practically hear her excitement crackling through the screen.

"Texts won't do this justice," I muttered, unlocking my phone to call her. It rang once before Gabby picked up, her voice bursting through like a campaign slogan.

"Libby! Give me the scoop! Is your place campaign-headquarters chic or lobbyist-lounge luxe?"

"Gabby, it's ridiculous," I declared, kicking off my heels and hopping onto a bar stool. "And there's enough closet space to hide a four-term senator's skeletons."

"Girl, if those skeletons can rock a pantsuit like you, I say let 'em out!" Gabby's laugh was infectious, a reminder of why she was my chief of friendship.

"Get over here. We've got to celebrate, and I need your brain for Operation: George Campaign Office Infiltration." My fingers drummed on the countertop, the rhythm of political plots forming in my head.

"Say no more, I'm grabbing my spy kit—and by that, I mean my killer instincts and a bottle of celebratory champagne. See you in a few!"

"See you in a few, Agent Jean." I grinned, ending the call and letting the buzz of anticipation fill my chest. With Gabby on my side, William Benjamin wouldn't stand a chance.

* * *

The door swung open, and there was Gabby, all wild curls and conspiratorial grin, a bottle of champagne dangling from her fingers like a campaign promise.

"Operation: Campaign Infiltration is officially underway," she announced, striding in with the confidence of a seasoned lobbyist on K Street.

I enveloped her in a hug, feeling the last of my solo jitters fade away. "So, tell me everything!" She plopped onto my new couch, her eyes gleaming with intrigue.

"The run was a success, I think."

"Okay," she urged with paws scratching for more.

"I only had to listen to him rattle on about tax reform for an hour," I said, hiding the fact that I actually enjoyed hearing his perspective.

"Listen, flatter him all the way," she said. "It doesn't matter how zany his ideas are. If you buy in, he'll be yours."

"Here's the kicker, though," I said, leaning in. "Midway through our run, his strategist came to tell him about the Caron financing."

"No way," she said.

"It seems they're drumming up a scheme with the Liberty

Action Committee."

"Maybe something to launder the funds?"

"Exactly," I said. "It sounds like they're aiming to have it done by the InterContinental event."

"Makes sense," she said. "That event is so important for them."

"He was secretive about it, so I knew exactly what he was talking about."

She hummed a second. "I wonder if you can get him to take you to that event."

"The InterContinental?"

"Yes! It'd be perfect. All the major players will be there. Imagine the dirt you could dig up in that den of vipers."

"Oh, that would be amazing," I said. "He's probably got some other bimbo to take."

"Libby, girl, you are the only one in his eyes right now."

"Well, for now, I'm setting my sights a bit lower," I said.

"Yes, so he invited you to the campaign office?"

"Mmhm, because he thinks I'm so interested in politics."

"Oh you two are so cute," she giggled. "Okay, so here's what you have to do."

She jumped as if she were a cat ready to pounce.

"You'll use that sharp tongue and sharper mind to talk shop with him—campaign strategies, voter demographics, the usual spiel. But then, oh-so-casually, shift the conversation towards finances. See if he is willing to tell you more about this scheme they're working on and, ideally, show you the ledger."

"Subtle as ever, Gabby." I chuckled, impressed by her strategic acumen. "I'm on it. He won't know what hit him."

"Exactly. But remember, Libby, this is, like 4D chess, girl."

"We're up to 4D now?"

"Oh yes. Keep it cool, collected, and utterly charming." Gabby's eyes were serious now, a strategist considering every angle of attack.

"Got it. Cool as a cucumber in a bowl of hot sauce." I flashed a grin, but I felt her caution settle in my chest. This was no small game; stakes were as high as stilettos on debate night.

She squeezed my hand and turned to the champagne. The pop was like a cathartic release after all the subterfuge I'd been gearing up for.

Gabby poured two glasses and we toasted to Mata Hari.

"Okay, this place is sooo cute," she said, bouncing her gaze around the interior.

"Come," I said, "you've got to see these suits!" And we skated into the bedroom.

CHAPTER 13

THE MOMENT I stepped into the lion's den, a.k.a. the George campaign office, my stomach churned with a mix of excitement and pure, unadulterated fear. The air buzzed with an energy that felt foreign yet electrifying, as if I had just plugged into an ideological socket opposite to my own.

"Miss Elizabeth Hart, as I live and breathe," came the smooth voice of William Benjamin, ever the charmer. His warm smile was like a lighthouse in stormy seas, and despite myself, I found my tension ebbing away.

"Mister William Benjamin," I greeted, managing a grin that didn't reveal the swarm of butterflies in my gut. "Fancy seeing you here."

He gestured grandly toward the interior of the office. "Care for a tour?"

As I followed him through the maze of sleek desks and glowing screens, I couldn't help but compare this well-oiled machine to the more makeshift battle stations I was used to. It was all clean lines and cool colors, each staffer laser-focused.

"Your setup here is . . . impressive," I admitted reluctantly, taking note of how every piece of technology seemed to be from some sci-fi future where campaigns were won by algorithms and drones.

"That's quite a compliment coming from a tech exec," William said with a proud nod.

"Right," I murmured, tucking a stray lock of hair behind my ear, a nervous tic that I hoped went unnoticed. I mentally nudged myself—time to shift gears and play the part Gabby and I had concocted.

"Speaking of getting the job done," I ventured, trying to sound casual, "I've heard these rumors about Caron's financial involvement. Must be quite the boon having that level of support."

William's eyes flickered to mine, a hint of steel beneath his easygoing facade. "Rumors are the currency of D.C., Elizabeth. But let's focus on what's on the table, shall we? For example, our digital marketing team is doing wonders with targeted ads."

I nodded, schooling my features to mask the frustration simmering within. So much for the direct approach. Time to regroup and think of a new angle—a way to charm or perhaps outwit information out of him. After all, if there's one thing I've learned in politics, it's that there's always another way to spin the story.

* * *

"Marketing, huh? I suppose that's where the real magic happens," I said, steering William toward a topic that I assumed was safer than the treacherous waters of campaign finance.

"Exactly!" William exclaimed. He led me to a group of staffers huddled around an array of screens, their furrowed brows rivaling the complexity of the data analytics displayed before them. "We're trying to figure out the best approach to reach undecided voters aged forty to fifty-five. It's a tough nut to crack."

"Ah, the elusive swing voter," I said, eyeing the charts and graphs that might as well have been hieroglyphics for all the sense they made to me.

But then something struck me. This was something that we had worked on at the Charlie Archer campaign. And we not only had the same problem, but we solved it with a fresh new strategy.

I suddenly had the urge to show off and tell William and his team all about it.

"The X Factor . . . ," I muttered.

Everyone looked at me with alarm. As soon as they did, I knew I had said too much. They were on to me.

"What's that?" William asked.

"Eh, the X Factor," I said, dancing a bit around my place as if to distract from my blunder. "Haven't you heard of the X Factor?"

The staffers all shook their heads.

"In my last job . . . ," I started, "we discovered this important insight."

They all glared at me as if I had the key to unlock all of their hopes and dreams.

"It turned out to be the deciding factor in convincing Generation X voters—eh, consumers—to buy."

It was like light bulbs went on in each of their heads. I knew this is exactly what they needed, and I also knew that it was the last thing I should be telling them.

One staffer, with a pencil perpetually stuck behind his ear, turned to me with a hopeful gaze. "You wouldn't happen to remember this insight, would you?"

I panicked. I would have loved nothing more than to talk about my past work, but it would have basically been giving the enemy our best stuff. What if they employed the same approach and used it to win?

"Me?" I feigned surprise. The challenge was too tempting, and my mind buzzed with the thrill of strategizing. But I couldn't hand over the secrets, especially given the fact that I was supposed to be gathering secrets from them. "No, that was so long ago," I said, and looked for their reactions. They didn't buy it.

"Proprietary knowledge!" William boomed, inciting everyone to laugh. "We totally understand!"

I sighed out a laugh of relief. That was a close one.

"But," he said, "if you ever want a job in politics, you have one here."

"I'll keep it in mind," I said, grinning.

"Sure, sure," he nodded, his smile saying he knew the score just as well as I did.

As we wrapped up the tour, the office buzzing with newfound energy, I couldn't help the twinge of guilt tugging at my conscience. Here I was, supposed to be digging for dirt, and, instead, I was giving them the gold. Vanessa Martinez would have a field day if she ever found out.

"Thanks for the tour, Sir William. It has been . . . illuminating," I said, shaking his hand with a firmness that belied my internal turmoil.

"Anytime, Elizabeth. But, seriously, we could use someone like you on the team." His grin was like a secret handshake we'd inadvertently created. "If you ever have a hankering to get into the fray, you're welcome to jump in here."

If only you knew, William Benjamin, if only.

Stepping out into the crisp D.C. air, the weight of my predicament settled on my shoulders. No intel on the ledger, no closer to exposing whatever George had up his sleeve. Just a head full of what-ifs and a niggling suspicion that I might've just given the enemy everything.

"Great work, Hart," I muttered under my breath, sarcasm lacing my words. "Next time, try not to be so darned helpful."

CHAPTER 14

I FUMBLED WITH my phone, the screen a glaring beacon of my anxiety as I punched in Gabby's number. The ringing gnawed at my insides until her voice, a soothing balm of calm and reason, wrapped around me.

"Libby, what's up? You sound like you're trying to defuse a bomb."

"Close," I said, pacing my cramped apartment, "I think I might've accidentally armed one." My words tumbled out, rapid-fire, as I recounted my slip-up at the George campaign headquarters.

"Java Jolt, pronto," Gabby suggested without missing a beat.

"See you in ten," I replied, already on the way to my car, ready to go.

The bell above the coffee shop door jingled its judgment as I pushed through, instantly spotting Gabby, stretched across her chair like a panther ready to pounce.

"What happened?" she commanded, sliding a steaming cup across the table to me.

"Okay, so picture this: I'm in enemy territory, right? Doing my best impression of James Bond ... minus the laser blasters," I began, wrapping my hands around the warmth of the mug, "but, instead, I end up in this marketing brainstorm session."

"Classic Libby luck," Gabby mused, her eyes twinkling with mischief.

"Exactly," I continued, feeling the heat rise to my cheeks. "And there's William Benjamin, Mr. Charming himself, introducing me to his team like I'm the answer to all their prayers. Get this. They're stuck on swing voters aged forty to fifty-five, Gabby—the very thing I wrestled with for Archer."

Gabby gasped. "The X Factor?"

"Mmmhm," I said, ashamed.

"Tell me you didn't hand them the playbook."

"Of course not!" I protested, a little too quickly. "Okay, maybe I let something small slip, but nothing major. I just ... ."

"Libs ... ," she said as a parent scolding her child.

"Well, I might have, maybe, sort of, mentioned the X Factor a little."

"You mentioned it?"

"Only just," I admitted, the weight of my slip-up pressing down on my chest. "It came out before I could barricade it behind my teeth."

"Libby!" Her exclamation was a half-scold, half-laugh, but with a gravity that rooted me to my chair.

"Did they know about it?"

"No, they thought I was talking about the reality show."

"Did you spill anything else?"

I shook my head, my locks bouncing around my shoulders

like agitated springs. "No, no. My lips were sealed tighter than a classified document after that. But just uttering those two words felt like arming the enemy with a secret weapon."

Gabby was bouncing her gaze around the objects on the table as if she were connecting dots. "This is perfect."

"Perfect?"

"Yes, Libs, look," she said, leaning forward, conspiratorial and keen. "I'm channeling my inner Vanessa here."

"That's not the most reassuring thing to hear, Gabs."

"Give it to him."

"Give it . . . ?"

"Yes, give him all of your insights and solutions."

"You're saying to just give the enemy everything we did to win those swing voters?"

"Yes," she said.

"That doesn't exactly feel like a winning strategy, Gabby."

"Libby Hart, political savant, sometimes you can't see the forest for the trees." She reached across the table, tapping a manicured nail against my wrist. "Remember, 5D chess."

"Gabby, I'm feeling like a pawn in three-inch heels," I said, though her confidence was starting to seep into my pores, emboldening me.

"Consider this," Gabby said, her tone now smooth as silk but with an edge sharp enough to slice through my doubts. "William hasn't been very open with you about the Caron financing, right?"

"Right," I said.

"Maybe he just needs to build more trust with you."

"Okay."

"And giving him your work on the X Factor is all kinds of trust—that's your Trojan horse. Once inside, you snag the Caron financing ledger."

"But those swing voters could give them the election in the end."

"But they won't have those voters after we leak the ledger," she said slowly as if to drive the point home.

And it all suddenly came together.

"Strategic intimacy," I echoed, letting the words roll off my tongue. They tasted like potential mixed with a hint of moral ambiguity.

"Exactly. You're not just cozying up to the enemy; you're infiltrating their defenses." Gabby's smile was all Cheshire Cat, and I found myself grinning back despite the unease that clung to me like a second skin.

"Damn," I thought out loud. "Forget 5D chess. This is more like 15D chess."

"All the Ds chess," she said.

"All the Ds."

"Trust me," Gabby winked, "the pieces will fall into place."

"I just feel so vulnerable thinking about giving him my best ideas."

"Every great political achievement thrives on the sharing of secrets, Libby," Gabby continued, stirring her chai latte with a vigor that suggested she was trying to whip up a love potion. "You can't spell 'collusion' without 'us.'"

I couldn't help but chuckle. "You're relentless," I said, shaking my head at her incorrigible spirit.

"You know it." Gabby grinned, satisfied.

As if right on cue, my phone buzzed against the wooden table, a surprising counterpoint to our intense scheming. I glanced at the screen, my heart hitching at William's name. The message was casual, almost nonchalant, but it felt like a loaded gun wrapped in a velvet glove.

"Speak of the devil," I muttered, showing Gabby the text. Her reaction was instantaneous, a squeal escaping her lips as she clapped her hands together.

"Libby! This is it!" she exclaimed.

I looked at the message. "'Madame President, I rise to introduce Senate Bill 789, also known as the Romantic Dinner at My Place on Friday Act.'"

I let out only half a laugh because the rest of me was so nervous as to almost throw up.

"Oh this is totally it, honey child," Gabby said.

"I just don't know if I can do this."

"Come on, you've danced with dragons before," Gabby teased, her enthusiasm infectious. "Just think of William as . . . a particularly handsome dragon."

"Charming and potentially fire-breathing," I conceded, tapping my fingers nervously on the table.

I punched out a response. "'The Senator from Washington D.C. has the floor.'"

"'Thank you. Senate Bill 789 allocates federal funds for the distribution of well-procured vittles at the domicile of the Senator from Washington D.C. along with magnificent conversation on the evening of Friday of this week at 7 p.m.'"

I shook my head at my phone, in disbelief at how adorable I found this man.

"Libs, if you don't walk out of his place with the ledger, I would be very surprised. He's practically giving it to you."

"Right," I said, contemplating a response. "Let's just hope I walk out of his place with my integrity intact as well."

"Operation Heartstrings is a go," Gabby declared, the words feeling like a pact with destiny. Or perhaps just a date with the most deliciously complicated man I'd ever met. Either way, it was going to be one hell of a show.

CHAPTER 15

I PULLED UP to William's townhouse and took my time peering at it as if on a recon mission. Really, I was just nervous and stalling. It was ironic. In all my escapades with William thus far, the time I felt most like a spy was when I was preparing to *give away* secret information.

Finally, I pulled myself out of my car and walked up the stairs to his door. I was so fretful that I actually stopped and looked at my phone for a minute before knocking.

Then the door opened. William gave me the biggest grin, not at all fazed by the fact that I must have looked like some weird canvasser lurking on his stoop.

"Miss Hart, party of two," he said, and waved me in.

I reacquainted myself with the gorgeous interior of his townhouse and let out a contented sigh.

"Ah, a nice choice," he commented, eyeing the label of the wine I brought.

"Only the best for Mister Benjamin," I said.

"I would expect nothing less," he said.

"I see Martin Van Buren's chandelier is doing well," I said.

"As always," he said with a grin. "Hope you're hungry," William said as he led me to a table set for two, candles flickering softly, casting a warm glow over the white linen and fine china.

"I didn't realize your townhouse was Michelin-starred," I replied, duly impressed.

He pulled out my chair and I sat down. "Only the best for Miss Hart," he said, scooting me into the table. Then he uncorked the wine and poured two oversized glasses as if he were the maître d'.

"If I didn't know you better, Mister Benjamin, I would suspect that you were trying to wine and dine me," I said with a sly smile.

"At least I'm not trying to nickel and dime you."

"That is apparent," I said, eyes widened as he brought out an impressive appetizer.

"But, seriously," he said, "I really would like to know more about the X Factor."

I gasped playfully. "Mixing business with pleasure, Mister Benjamin? I'm shocked!"

"I figured if there was anyone who wouldn't mind skipping the small talk, it was you."

"Accurate," I said, raising my glass for a toast. "To jumping straight into the deep end."

"To the deep end," he concurred, and tipped his glass to mine.

"I understand if you don't want to share trade secrets and all," he said, "but if you can lend some insights, I would be very appreciative."

I poked at my crab cake, contemplating how I would go about framing the conversation. Part of me wanted to simply tell him everything. Nothing would have made me happier than to tell him all about our successes at the Archer campaign. Of course, I couldn't do that. So, I had to be subtle.

"Okay, so, the X Factor—it's . . . ." I paused, choosing my words carefully. "It's based on the fact that Generation X is the smallest demographic, but they pack a punch." I jabbed my fork into the air for emphasis as if skewering a piece of political wisdom. "Since they're so skeptical, they are often undecided and ultimately serve as the deciding factor."

William's brow arched. "Especially in elections."

"Exactly!" The word burst from me with more enthusiasm than I'd intended. "It works for consumers, but it's almost more effective with voters."

"Interesting."

"So," I said, laying my hands on the table, "the question is how to connect with Gen X voters?"

"Yes, that's our big challenge."

"Well, we found that, since they're so skeptical, they tend to buy based on substance, not on any gimmicks. It has to be real."

"I hear you."

"For them, it's all about trust, right? No slick sales pitches. They want a candidate who's got integrity, principles, consistency. Pull that off, no lies, no mudslinging, and you've got their vote."

"Ah, so a clean campaign," William mused. "Sounds eerily similar to Charlie Archer's run."

My heart skipped a beat. "That's because . . . it is," I admitted, feeling a sudden prick of defensiveness. "Archer was onto something and he had won the swing vote and would have won the primary if he hadn't stepped on the establishment's toes."

"You seem to know an awful lot about the Archer campaign," he said.

I gulped down a swallow. "We did some consulting for them."

I think he believed me. "But your X Factor—there's real potential there."

"Potential?" I echoed.

"Absolutely. It could be a game-changer for Barry George." His eyes lit up, not unlike the way mine do when a plan starts to click together. "Elizabeth, this is ingenious."

"Is it now?" My cheeks flushed with a blend of pride and surprise.

"Imagine this," William began, his eyes gleaming with fervor. "A campaign that eschews the usual mudslinging and empty promises. We focus on George's unwavering dedication to his constituents, his unshakeable principles. We show the voters that he's not just another face in the crowd, but a beacon of honesty in a sea of corruption."

I nodded along, feeling the pieces fall into place like a perfectly crafted puzzle. "Yes, yes! We highlight his consistency, his refusal to play dirty politics." I was getting as excited as William. "I mean," I said, slowing down, "*you* highlight."

"I think that means you really want to join the team," he said.

I cocked my head with a smile. "No," I said. "I'll let you have all the fun."

"We're here if you ever change your mind."

I let the thought swim around in my head. It did sound amazing, the thrill of a daring strategy taking shape before my eyes and the cutest strategist in D.C. to work on it with.

I couldn't tear my gaze away from him, his eyes sparkling with a shared passion for this unorthodox approach. It was as though we were dance partners, gliding through the intricacies of political strategy with a perfect rhythm. His voice resonated with conviction and purpose, echoing my own beliefs like a harmonious melody.

As he painted a vivid picture of how Barry George's campaign could be transformed by our revolutionary idea, I found myself hanging on his every word. The way he spoke, so confident and determined, made me believe that together we could truly make a difference in the political landscape.

The air crackled with excitement, and I couldn't help but marvel at how effortlessly we connected despite our opposing affiliations. It was a revelation to realize that beneath the surface differences, William and I shared a profound understanding of what truly mattered in politics—integrity, honesty, and a genuine commitment to the people.

In that moment, surrounded by the elegant trappings of William's townhouse, I felt a sense of kinship with him that transcended party lines. It was as if the barriers that divided us politically had melted away, leaving behind a shared vision of a better, more honest political landscape.

As we delved deeper into our strategy for Barry George's campaign, I found myself entranced by the passion and creativity that William brought to the table. His ideas sparked a fire within me, igniting a newfound sense of purpose and determination.

Together, we crafted a narrative that centered on integrity and authenticity, daring to challenge the status quo and rewrite the rules of political engagement.

With each detail we mapped out, I couldn't help but admire the way William's mind worked—sharp, analytical, yet brimming with empathy and insight. It was like watching a master painter at work, creating a masterpiece of ideas and ideals that spoke to the very core of what I believed in.

"Charlie Archer," I found myself confessing, "I mean, he's a Democrat, but he's one Democrat I could've worked for. Integrity, honesty. I think no matter what your political persuasion, you could support that."

"He was one hell of a candidate," William agreed. "You know, I think even I could work for him."

I gasped. "William Benjamin, closet Democrat?" I couldn't help but chuckle.

"Let's not get carried away," he shot back with a grin. "Maybe if he were an Independent."

The laughter that followed was a duet of shared understanding, a momentary truce in our political tug-of-war. And just like that, under the soft glow of William's dining room chandelier, I found myself appreciating the unexpected common ground we stood upon.

* * *

Leaning back in my chair, I tried to look casual, even though my mind was racing like a caffeinated squirrel. "So, if you go with the X Factor strategy," I ventured, tapping my fingers on the stem of my wine glass, "wouldn't you need to make changes?"

"Changes?"

"Yes," I said, trying my best to be subtle. "If you ran on integrity, you'd have to clean up that Caron financing issue, wouldn't you?"

He looked at me almost as if he were scolding me.

"I don't know," he said, "it's only an issue because the Democrats are overly worried about it."

"Yes, but there's good reason to be, isn't there?"

"It's not that big of a deal," he said. "All candidates have their sketchy financing. Even Peats has his share of dubious donors."

"He does?"

"Oh sure. But you don't hear about that because we Republicans don't care about it."

"Hmmph," I mumbled.

"And anyway, it won't even be an issue once Simon's ledger is done."

"Simon?" My eyebrow quirked up. "Isn't he the one who gets nervous around staplers?"

"Only when they're loaded," William said, chuckling. "But, yes, he should have it done by the InterContinental event."

"I've heard of this InterContinental event."

"It's our biggest event of the year," he said, "all of the biggest players will be there. It'll be a feast for policy wonks."

"Sounds like fun."

"Yeah, if you don't mind fuzzy-browed lawmakers chewing your ear for hours," he said. "This year's theme is masquerade, which will make it entertaining at least."

"Ooh," I said, eyebrows bouncing up and down.

"Yep. Masks, mystery, and major players of Washington all under one roof." He took a sip of his wine, watching me over the rim. "The only thing that could make it bearable . . . ," he said, and paused. I flicked up an eyebrow. "Might you be interested in being my guest?"

"Me?" I feigned shock, pressing a hand to my chest. "Mingle with the high-and-mighty of the GOP? How could a girl resist?"

"Seriously, Elizabeth." His tone softened, and there was an earnest glint in his eyes. "It would mean a lot to have you there with me."

The thought had its appeal—glamorous gowns, whispered conversations behind ornate masks, dancing with William while the rest of the room faded into obscurity. But the reminder lingered, sharp as the cut of my steak: this was enemy territory.

"Certainly, I'm not exactly . . . ," I hesitated, searching for the right way to phrase it without blowing my cover.

"Political?" he finished for me, a playful smirk tugging at his lips. "All the better. You'd be a refreshing contrast to the run of the mill."

My mind flicked to Vanessa's words about dedication to the cause. Was this crossing a line, or was it just another step in the intricate dance of bazillion-D chess?

"All you'd need is a mask," he said, and then nearly leapt to correct himself. "Oh, and a gown. You'll need a dress too. It's not going to be one of those *Illuminati* masquerades."

I laughed. "Hmm, what kind of girl do you think I am?"

He sighed in attempt to hide his embarrassment. "Anyway, so you'll come?"

I leaned in toward him with a huge smile. "I'd love to."

"Great," William agreed, his gaze lingering on mine, a promise of more than just political allegiances hanging between us.

* * *

After dinner, he walked me out to my car and we embraced for what might have been the tenderest kiss I've ever experienced. As I drove home, I recalled our conversation, the way he listened intently to every word I said, his genuine interest in my thoughts and ideas. The spark between us was undeniable, crackling in the air like electricity.

Once home, the romance of the evening's events played on a loop in my mind, each moment with William etched vividly like a painting in my memory. The way he held my gaze, the way he lighted up when we were talking strategy, and the subtle warmth that lingered in his eyes—it was all a kaleidoscope of sensations I had never experienced before.

As I stood before the mirror, shedding the elegant facade of the night and slipping into the comfort of my pajamas, a whirlwind of emotions swirled within me. The question nagged at me like an insistent whisper in the quiet of my room: What did it all mean?

Could this be more than just politics and pretend? Was there a deeper connection brewing beneath the surface, yearning to be acknowledged? I paced back and forth, fragmented thoughts colliding like stars in a cosmic dance. William's sincerity, his unwavering dedication to integrity—how could that not stir something within me that had long been dormant?

The weight of Vanessa's words about dedication to the cause pressed on my mind, like a heavy cloak I couldn't shrug off. Was I willing to continue this charade, weaving a tapestry of deception even as my heart tugged me in a different direction? Or did I need to come clean and face the consequences with the only man I'd fallen for?

CHAPTER 16

'I CAN'T DO IT!!!!!!!!' I texted Gabby.

The fifty-five exclamation points were a little dramatic, I admit. But they accurately reflected my inner struggle.

'Are you at your condo?'

'Yes,' I replied.

'B there in 15.'

I was curled up in my bed, unable to escape the cozy dream-like state I had been in since waking up.

With Gabby on her way, I finally pulled myself out of bed and got dressed.

When she got there, she didn't even give me a hello hug. "What's this about 'Can't do it'?" she said as she buzzed in and started making coffee.

"Oh Gabby."

"Oh boy," she said. "How did it go down?"

"It started out straightforward enough," I reported. "I gave him the details on the X Factor and he took off from there. He was coming up with all these amazing ideas on how he'd implement it in his campaign. It was like we were working together on it."

"Uh huh," she said, suspicious. "Did you get the ledger?"

"They're going to have it at the InterContinental event."

"Which he's going to take you to?"

I nodded. "It's a masquerade ball."

"Oooh, girl, that sounds delectable."

"I just . . . ," I sighed, unable to get the vision of him out of my mind.

She watched how I talked about him and shook her head. "Girl, you are in love."

"No."

"Mmhm, yeah. You're certifiable."

I shook my head, unable to lose the smile on my face.

"So you don't think you can go through with this," she concluded.

"I have to tell him," I said.

"Don't even think about it."

"But I can't continue on lying like this. Maybe I just tell him that I'm a centrist."

"You know what will happen if you do, don't you?"

I nodded, contemplating the inevitable.

"Everything will fall apart. And there's no way he'll give you that ledger."

"Maybe he'd still be interested."

"Ain't nobody like William Benjamin gon be messin' with some centrist Democrat."

"Especially one who has been lying to him in order to get his secret files."

"Exactly, girl."

"He did say that he would consider working for a guy like Charlie Archer," I said, shrugging.

"Sounds like a hypothetical, girl. He's chief of staff of one of the most powerful Republicans in Congress. He's not going to defect."

"No," I said, dreamily.

"No ma'am. We're too close," Gabby said. "You can go tell him all your dark secrets and you two can go run off to Puerto Rico and start a third party, but not until we've got that ledger."

"Yeah."

"He said they'd have it by the InterContinental event?"

"Yep."

"Well, you're going to have to make quite the splash at the InterContinental, then aren't you?"

I nodded, sure she was right, but somehow incapable of believing it.

"You know what you need?" she asked, conspiratorially.

"Tell me."

"Retail therapy," she said, grabbing my hand and angling for the door. "We need to find you an ensemble worthy of this prestigious gala."

I breathed in deeply as if to convince myself and nodded. In a flash, we were off.

* * *

The moment Gabby and I stepped into the boutique, a buzz

of excitement fizzed through my veins like champagne. I was still disconsolate because of my quagmire with William, but the sight of the stylish masks and fancy accouterments filled me with anticipation of the glamorous event. Sequins glittered from every corner, satin whispered secrets of elegance, and feathers promised a dance of mystery. Gabby was practically vibrating next to me, her wild curls bouncing as she clapped her hands together.

"I don't know why the Republicans get to have all the fun," she said. "We're over here having pizza parties for block walks. They're throwing lavish masquerade balls."

"The price we pay for hating capitalism," I needled.

I bit my lip as we wove through the racks of gowns, my heart dancing an odd step.

"Dang, girl," she said, "I'm finna switch parties over here just so I can get all Eyes Wide Shut on some tuxedoed billionaires."

"They wouldn't be able to handle you, my darling," I said, and then I spotted it—a display of masks so intricate and stunning, they could've been crafted by whimsical sprites with too much time on their hands. Velvet, lace, jewels—they beckoned me closer, each one a promise of glamor and intrigue.

"Try this one!" Gabby thrust a feathered creation into my hands, all deep blues and greens, a peacock's dream.

Slipping it over my eyes, I felt a jolt of someone else's confidence—someone daring and bold. "How do I look?" I asked, turning towards Gabby.

"Like a bird of paradise," she declared, but her eyes were already scanning for another option. "Gorgeous, but not quite

. . . it."

Mask after mask graced my face, each more elaborate than the last. A golden sunburst that made me feel like a queen; a silver filigree that whispered of moonlit secrets; a black lace number that hinted at midnight rendezvous.

"Stop the press, try this one!" Gabby handed me a mask adorned with tiny crystals that caught the light like a handful of stars had crashed into me.

Placing it over my eyes, something clicked. The weight of it felt right, like it was made just for me. My reflection showed a woman ready for battle, armed with charm and wit.

"Damn, Libby," Gabby breathed out, her approval evident. "That's the one. You look like a constellation come down to play politics."

"Then let's hope the stars align for the ball," I dreamed, a smile curving my lips behind the mask.

* * *

The next stop was at a designer store down the street, which itself felt like a betrayal of my proletarian personality. Stepping into the gown section felt like wading into enemy territory, a sea of rich fabrics and ornaments that I'd sworn to resist. But, just as I was about to turn and leave, I saw something that appeared to be calling my name.

A red satin gown, draped over a sleek mannequin, glowing like a siren's beacon amidst the sober hues. Gabby caught a glimpse of my expression and chuckled.

"Come on, Lib," she urged, her voice wrapped in the silk of persuasion. "You've got to admit, it's jaw-dropping."

"Jaw-droppingly partisan," I muttered, the weight of my Democrat blue heart anchoring me to the spot. The red of the gown screamed Republican, the color of Barry George's ties and campaign banners, yet the cut, the fall of the fabric—it whispered secrets of power and seduction.

"Libby 'Bleeding' Hart in Republican red," Gabby mused, cocking her head to one side. "Now that would be a bold strategy."

"Bold or betraying?" I questioned, the words leaving a tart taste in my mouth. But then, the image of William's smile flickered in my mind—open, honest, infectiously enthusiastic about our campaign strategies. He would want nothing more than to see me in this.

"Sometimes, you've got to cross the aisle to win the vote," Gabby said, tapping the dress as if calling a close race. She was right; politics made strange bedfellows, and, if a red gown was my ticket to the inner circle, then so be it.

"Fine," I sighed, snatching the hanger with a dramatic flourish. "But if I start talking about bootstraps, stage an intervention."

"Deal," Gabby agreed, grinning like she'd just brokered international peace.

In the changing room, doubts buzzed around my head like pesky flies as I slipped out of my clothes and into the gown. My reflection in the mirror gave me pause—a stranger draped in the enemy's colors. Yet, something shifted within me, a tectonic plate of self-perception moving to reveal a new landscape of confidence.

"Wow," I breathed out, the word feeling small compared to the transformation. The gown hugged every curve with the precision of a political strategist lining up votes. It wasn't just red; it was power, it was allure, it was sexy as hell—it was me, redefined.

"Let's see then!" Gabby called out, impatience lacing her tone.

I stepped out, half-expecting a drum roll. Gabby's eyes went wide, her lips parting in a silent 'O' of awe. "Holy battleground state, Libby! You don't just look hot—you're a freaking wildfire!"

"Is that good?" I teased, giving a twirl that sent the skirt dancing around me like flames.

"Good?" Gabby laughed. "Girl, you're going to burn down the house at this ball. William won't know what hit him."

"Maybe he's got good insurance," I quipped, the thrill of anticipation bubbling in my chest. I felt invincible, like I could sway a senate vote with a side step.

"Red might just become your new favorite color," Gabby said, her approval warming me more than any campaign trail ever could.

"Let's not get carried away," I countered, my voice light but my heart heavy with the gravity of what I was about to do. This gown wasn't just fabric and thread; it was a promise of victory, a whisper of scandal, and maybe, just maybe, a chance at something more with William.

CHAPTER 17

THE DAY OF the masquerade, I could barely hold my coffee mug, my nerves made me so jittery. So, I did what any red-blooded, blue-minded runner would do—I laced up my running shoes and set out for an extra-long run.

The cool breeze brushed against my cheeks as I set off, each stride bringing me closer to a sense of clarity and purpose.

The rhythmic sound of my footfalls echoed through the quiet streets, a hypnotic beat that seemed to drown out the doubts and fears swirling in my mind. As I passed by iconic landmarks and historic buildings, I felt a surge of energy coursing through my veins, propelling me forward with renewed determination.

The rising sun painted the sky in bipartisan hues of red and blue with sparkly gold in between, casting a warm glow over the city awakening to another day. With every breath I took, I could feel the tension melting away, leaving behind a sense of calm resolve.

As I reached the steps of the Capitol building, I paused to take in the grandeur of its towering columns and majestic dome. A sense of awe washed over me, reminding me of the magnitude of the work I had engaged in, the delicate dance of power and influence that shaped our nation's future. I straightened my shoulders, the weight of responsibility settling comfortably on them.

Turning back towards my apartment, I quickened my pace, my thoughts already drifting to the evening ahead. I knew the masquerade ball was all about political maneuvering, but, if I were honest with myself, I knew that all I really cared about was seeing William. His easy smile and quick wit had already begun to chip away at the walls I had carefully constructed around my heart. This was going to be quite a night.

* * *

My average getting ready time before going out was around a half hour. I had always prided myself on being low-mainte-nance. But that night, I was the Princess of Luxembourg on a royal tour.

I twisted in front of the full-length mirror, the red fabric of my dress clinging to every curve like it had been painted on. The masquerade mask perched precariously in my hands, feathers and sequins winking at me as if they were in on the joke. For a moment, I hardly recognized the woman staring back at me from the glass—a more feminine creature than Libby Hart, the political pit bull, was ever meant to be.

"Who knew vulnerability could look so damn good?" I muttered to my reflection. It was a risky play, this softening of edges. But tonight's charade required finesse over force, and I was ready to act the part.

The doorbell chimed, and I felt a trill of something unexpected. Delight. I wasn't thinking about the spy games or the ledger. I was just excited to see William in a tuxedo. I took one final assessing glance in the mirror and headed for the door.

William stood on the other side, and when I swung the door wide, his sharp intake of breath was audible. His eyes—which I'd seen calculate political moves with merciless precision—now swept over me with undisguised awe.

"Elizabeth, you look . . . incredible," he said, the corners of his mouth lifting in a half-smile that somehow managed to be both boyish and entirely disarming.

"Red is the color of power, or so I've been told," I noted, stepping into the hallway. "It seems to have struck you speechless, which I'll count as a win."

He offered his arm, a move so gallant it bordered on quaint, and led me to his car parked at the curb. William held the door open for me, and I slid into the leather seat with a grace I didn't know I possessed.

I couldn't help but smile as William opened the car door for me, a small gesture that spoke volumes about his character. My past boyfriends had never been so chivalrous; they were more concerned with signaling their feminism than treating me like a lady.

William was completely different, with his polished manners and debonair charm. As we drove through the city streets, I couldn't shake the fluttering sensation in my chest. It felt like

I was living out a fairy tale, with a knight in shining armor by my side. And though I knew it was all just a masquerade, I couldn't help but hope that this prince would stand by me even when the masks came off.

* * *

The car rolled up in front of the InterContinental, the grand building illuminated by a cascade of lights that turned the night into day. Valets bustled about, opening doors and ushering guests with practiced ease as we stepped onto the crimson carpet that unfurled like a river of velvet beneath our feet.

The air hummed with excitement, mingling scents of perfume and cologne in a heady mix. Laughter and conversation floated towards us, punctuated by the clinking of glasses and the soft strains of music drifting from within. I felt a surge of anticipation coursing through me, my pulse quickening as we made our way towards the entrance.

William looked every bit the leading man, his presence commanding attention as he escorted me through the throng of elegantly dressed attendees. Heads turned as we passed, whispers trailing in our wake like gossamer threads.

The grand ballroom unfolded before me like a scene from an old Hollywood movie, except the stars were politicos in tuxedos and glittering gowns, not actors. I adjusted my mask, an ornate supernova of a thing that somehow made me feel more daring than concealed. The rich reds and golds of the decor, the chandeliers dripping with crystals, and the champagne flutes catching the light in sparkling bursts—all of it was more lavish than any Democratic fundraiser I'd attended.

As we sauntered into the ballroom, William's magnetic presence drew an immediate crowd. People swarmed around him, eager to shake his hand and exchange pleasantries. With a charming smile, he introduced me to the sea of faces before us, each person a puzzle piece in this intricate political landscape. I greeted them with practiced ease, matching their enthusiasm with a hint of intrigue in my eyes.

"Come," William said, with a flick of his head, "I want you to meet Barry."

The senator was the only one without a mask on in a swarm of buzzing people. When he saw us approach, he stepped out of the group to greet us.

"Barry, allow me to introduce Miss Elizabeth Hart," William said, shaking the senator's hand and holding out his other hand to invite me in.

"It's such a pleasure to meet you," he said like honey.

I shook his hand firmly and took off my mask as I replied, "The pleasure is mine, Senator. I am a great admirer." I had to say it, of course, but the way William had touted his ideas and the grace he radiated made me almost believe the sentiment myself.

A knowing smile tugged at the corners of his lips as he murmured, "Ah, now I see why Will has spoken nonstop about you."

My face turned as red as my dress and I looked over to William as if to scold him. "Surely, you must not believe every-thing he says, Senator," I said.

The exchange felt like a dance, each step carefully calcu-lated to charm and disarm.

Barry George chuckled, a rich sound that filled the space between us. "Oh, I assure you, Miss Hart, Will's praise of you is well-deserved. It's refreshing to see someone who is *not* involved in politics enchanting us so."

I know he was being kind, but I also freaked out a little that he might have emphasized the 'not' because he was on to me.

"Thank you for your kind words, Senator," I replied diplo-matically.

As we chatted, our conversation peppered with light banter and political pleasantries, I was slightly startled to see Vanessa step into the periphery.

I was even more startled when she dipped into our circle. "Congratulations," she said almost as if it were to no one.

"Well," the senator said, welcoming her in, "if it isn't our favorite consultant on the other side."

"Senator, Mister Benjamin," she said, sharp as a shark.

"Miss Martinez," William said, "that sounds dangerously close to conceding the race with that congratulations."

"Close but no cigar," she said. "No, I was merely congratu-lating you on the lovely event. It's always a winner."

"Vanessa Martinez," William said, holding his hand out toward her, "this is Elizabeth Hart."

I shook her hand without a word, nervous that even small talk could give me away.

"She is new to D.C.," the senator said, "so don't go scaring her off with your wild policy ideas."

"Oh, I won't, any more than the standard from this crowd," she said, looking around at all the Republicans.

William turned to me. "Would you mind if I spoke with the senator a moment?"

"Not at all," I said, and they walked off, leaving me alone with Vanessa.

"So, you're new to D.C.?" she asked, eyeing William and the senator who were still in earshot.

"Yes, I got here in March," I replied.

Vanessa gestured that we walk a bit in the other direction. Once we were far enough from others, she changed her tone.

"Listen," she said, "Benjamin's colleague Simon Katz has the ledger."

"Oh, isn't that interesting?" I said, glancing around to make sure no one was close enough to hear. "And here I thought he only collected dull policy reports."

"Charming as ever," Vanessa said, dragging me closer with a hand on my arm. "Get it from him. Tonight. We're going to leak it for the big C-SPAN interview tomorrow."

"Consider it done," I whispered back, feeling the weight of the task settle on my shoulders.

"Good girl," Vanessa nodded once, then took a step back and scanned my ensemble. "You're a knockout," she said, and then melted back into the throng of guests.

* * *

I was perusing a mountain of culinary delights in the center of the ballroom when I felt a hand on the small of my back. I smiled and turned around, thinking it was William, but shocked to see it was Simon.

"Oh, Simon," I said, and slipped my back away from his hand. "I didn't know you were here."

"Please, call me Katz," he said. Was he trying to be funny?

"Oh, okay," I said, searching for William.

"So, I was surprised when I heard William invited you," he said while fiddling with his hands.

"Oh, why is that?"

"This is a pretty big deal," he said, "not for the uninitiated."

"Well, what makes you think I haven't been initiated?" I said, trying to keep it light.

"I saw you talking with that woman," Simon said, jerking his head in the direction of where we had been.

"Yes?"

"That is Vanessa Martinez, one of the highest paid Democrat consultants in D.C."

"You don't say," I teased. "And she seemed so nice."

"Well, looks can be deceiving," he said. "Just be careful around her."

"I really appreciate you keeping an eye out for me," I said.

"Oh, I've been watching you since you got here," he said.

Gulp. What the hell creep was this guy?

"So . . . " said, scrambling for a way to respond with civility. "Did you take care of that financing issue you were talking with William about the other day?"

"What?" he said, but then it hit him. "Oh, you mean the Caron financing scheme?"

"Oh is that what it's called?" I played dumb.

"Yes, after Didier Caron, the billionaire," he said, suddenly a flood of information. "You see, the Democrats want to make a big deal about the fact that Caron is financing the senator's campaign, but we figured out a way to obscure his donations so they can't track it." He was starting to sweat he was so excited.

"How did you manage that?"

"It is really ingenious," he said, and pulled out his tablet to show me. "Look, this is the ledger."

The ledger!

"All we did was to create a bunch of fake people, donated the money to the PAC under their names, and then the PAC sent the money to us."

I was watching wide-eyed as Simon relayed the information, amazed that he was actually sharing it at all, and that they had devised such an elaborate scheme to make it work.

"This is really amazing," I said. "Did you figure this out?"

He stuck his chest out. "Why, yes, in fact, I did."

"You're really smart," I said, putting my hand on his lapel.

"I know," he said without so much as a snigger.

"Say, I would love to be able to study this in detail," I said. "Can you send it to me?"

"Oh," he said, looking puzzled. "That's not something that we . . . ."

I started breathing heavily, thinking I might have overstepped my bounds.

"If you want, we can look at it together at my place later," he said, placing his hand on my back again. Was he actually coming on to me?

"Eh," I said, spinning around to distance myself from the creep. "I don't think William would appreciate that."

"Oh, he's fine if you see it, as long as I'm with you," he said.

I started searching for William everywhere in the ballroom. "That's not what I meant," I said, finally spotting William, talking with what looked like a bunch of wealthy donors. I tried to step away from Simon, but he kept stepping closer. "I have to . . . ," I tried, scanning the room again until my gaze fell on something I didn't expect to see at all—it was Gabby's friend Amanda, who was walking up to William at that very moment.

"I have to find William," I almost shouted. "See you later," I said and finally broke free on a mission to intercept Amanda before she could blow my cover. My heart raced as I weaved through the bodies.

* * *

"Hey, Elizabeth Hart! I remember you!" A voice boomed, halting my frantic pace. Congressman Marty Jenkins, whom I had met earlier, blocked my path, a wall of pinstriped suit and booming self-importance.

"Congressman Jenkins," I forced a smile, "lovely to see you again."

"Tell me," he droned on, oblivious to my barely concealed distress, "what's your take on the upcoming vote? They say it'll be tight, tighter than a . . . ."

I tuned out the rest, nodding mechanically while my attention fixed on Amanda, who had now reached William. They were talking, and every casual gesture they shared sliced through me.

"Elizabeth?" Jenkins's voice clawed back my focus.

"Right, the vote," I stammered, "tight as a drum, indeed." I scanned the room, desperate for an escape route, any distraction that would free me from this conversational quagmire.

"Ha! Drum, good one!" Jenkins chortled, slapping his knee. "You definitely have a way with words."

"Thank you," I said, backing away slowly, "but if you'll excuse me, I really must—"

"Of course, of course," he said, waving me off with grandiose magnanimity. "Go mingle! That's what these shindigs are for, after all!"

"Shindigs," I echoed faintly, seizing my chance. I plunged back into the tide of masked faces, my heels clicking a staccato rhythm against marble floors. I sidestepped a couple locked in a tango, ducked under a waiter's tray, and finally broke free from the crowd.

"Ah, there you are!" William's voice boomed as I approached, pulling me into the orbit of his charismatic presence. "We were just talking about you."

"Talking about me?" I feigned surprise, hoping my voice didn't betray the panic that had set my pulse racing moments ago.

"Absolutely," Amanda said. "I was surprised to find out that the darling of the ball just happened to be our own Libby Hart."

"Darling of the ball?" I stuttered, mortified.

"Just a little nickname we came up with," she said. "I was over there watching Mister Benjamin and I said, 'Who is that stunner with him?' And lo-and-behold, William tells me that I know her."

"Well, you don't know me, know me," I said, trying to guard against a potential bombshell.

"Oh, sure I do," she said, "we go way back, don't we?"

I bounced my wide eyes from her to William as if to warn her not to say anything, but she was so wiggly that I doubt she even noticed.

"We go back all the way to that one happy hour," I said.

"This is like a little reunion," she said, laughing.

"Yes, this is our happy hour anniversary," I chimed. William just stood by smiling.

"Don't worry," she said, "I'm not mad that you stole my boy-friend here."

My stomach fell to the floor. Surely she was joking.

"I knew that you would be a better match for William here from the moment I saw him."

"Oh yeah?"

"Of course—you're like ten times more attractive than me," she said.

"Stop it," I said.

"And, then there's the political angle."

Again, my stomach fell.

"I'm a flaming liberal Democrat, and, of course, you're as conservative as Republicans come," she said. As she spoke, I wasn't sure if I was hearing what I heard or if I were just wishing that she said it.

But no, she actually said I was conservative. Then she winked, so I knew she was playing along. "If only I had known that William was a Republican, I would have totally lied about my politics to get him in the sack."

I gulped down a swallow, uncertain that I could even manage a response.

"Elephants over donkeys, any day," she said, earning a chuckle from William.

"Speaking of time," William said, glancing at his wristwatch, the gold catching the light as he moved. "I have to exchange a few words with Simon before we head out."

"Well continue the reunion without you," I said, watching him stride away, every inch the gentleman-politician. I turned back to Amanda, my gratitude simmering beneath my composed exterior. "Amanda, you're a lifesaver. How did you know?"

"Vanessa Martinez gave me the heads-up earlier," she confessed, her tone casual, but her gaze sharp. "Said you might need a little backup. Looks like she was right."

"Vanessa," I repeated, a smile tugging at my lips despite the chaos of the night. "Well, thank her for me, will you? And yourself—I owe you big time."

"Consider it strategic investment," Amanda said with a

wink, just as William returned, his expression apologetic.

"Well, my lady, I think we've done enough schmoozing for the season," he said, offering his arm with the same chivalry that had swept me off my feet earlier.

"For a lifetime," I assured him, looping my arm through his, and we made our way toward the exit.

"Simon said he had told you about the Liberty Action Committee ledger," William said, almost as an aside.

I looked at him, startled. "Yes, it sounds like an interesting solution to the Caron financing issue," I said, unsure I could play it cool.

"He said you asked him to send it."

Uh oh. Was he on to me? "Yes," I tried. "I'd love to see how you worked it out."

"Yeah, he said he didn't want to send it to you because he didn't know you," he said.

"Yeah, makes sense," I said.

"He even went so far as to suggest that you are a Democrat spying on us," he said with an exaggerated laugh.

I tried to laugh along with him, but I was so nervous that I only let out a little wheezing.

"But I told him that I know you and that you are definitely not a Democrat."

"You did?"

"Anyway, I told him to send it to you. So you should have it in your email. I'd love to hear what you have to say about it."

I sighed. Could he really be that trusting of me? Suddenly, I felt the weight of my lies bear down on me. Even though it would seem that I would finally get the file I had been after all along, it felt as if I were farther than ever from my true goal.

CHAPTER 18

AS WILLIAM DROVE me to my condo, I reclined back into my seat, exhausted from the whirlwind of an event and my close calls at being discovered. And, now that we were done with all of that and I had the ledger, all I wanted to do was to sink into my bed and forget everything.

Of course, through it all, William was there for me, praising me in front of every high roller in D.C., and defending me against anyone who even looked at me askance. He was the most chivalrous gentleman a girl could ask for. If he only knew.

I put my hand on his neck and ran it through his hair a bit just to be able to touch him. He glanced over happily, like a schoolboy after the bell had rung.

He pulled into my condo and parked in front. Of course he walked me to my door and I paused before opening.

"Would you like to come in?" I said. "For a nightcap and superb conversation?"

"Now that is a proposition that I just can't pass on," he said.

With a chuckle, I led him into the condo. The click of the door shutting behind us resonated like a starting gun, and my stomach did that little nervous flutter. I was good at keeping cool under political fire, but William—William was an unexpected variable in my new life.

"Nice place," he commented, glancing around the condo with a curious tilt to his brow. "Surprisingly tidy for someone who just moved to D.C."

"Thanks," I said, trying to downplay the fact that I hadn't moved a thing. "What would you like to drink?" The bottles lined up in front of me seemed more daunting than facing a room full of hostile constituents.

"They say you can tell the quality of a bartender by the quality of her old fashioned." He leaned against the counter, all easy charm and politico grace.

"Do they say that?" I flashed what I hoped was a disarming smile. "Maybe you should make them. I'm not the world's best old-fashioned maker."

"Challenge accepted." William rolled up his sleeves, revealing forearms that could probably stir martinis and hearts with equal finesse. I swallowed, watching him assess my bar.

"Do I have everything you need?" I asked, arms outstretched.

"Mmmm," he muttered. "Do you ever?"

As he busied himself with muddling and mixing, I fished out my phone, thinking I'd turn on some music. My thumb hovered over the screen—Gabby's last message burning a hole in my conscience. 'I'm with Vanessa let me know if you've got it.'

I took a deep breath, anxious to even correspond with her, but I knew I at least had to let them know. I typed quickly, betraying my nerves. 'Got it.'

'Great send it to Vanessa ASAP,' Gabby shot back.

I grimaced. I knew what sending the ledger would mean. And it was basically a political death sentence to the gentleman making me a cocktail, the man who had treated me better than anyone had previously treated me in my entire life, the man who I had childishly envisioned as the father of my children on not a few occasions. Yeah, I didn't think I could quite send that ledger so soon.

"Everything okay?" William glanced over his shoulder, a half-cocked grin on his face as he shook a cocktail mixer with more gusto than necessary. "These aren't going to be typical old fashioneds."

"Yep, just . . . work stuff." A lie by omission, but then, wasn't my whole presence here one big act of subterfuge?

"New fashioneds," he said, with a hokey smile to boot.

Buzz. It was Vanessa now, her text as sharp and commanding as her tailored suits. 'Libby, I need that ledger.'

I couldn't even bear opening the message because as soon as I did I would need to reply with the file.

"What kind of music do you like?" I deflected.

"Oldies," he said, "of course."

"Of course," I repeated, scanning Pandora for it. "What, like Bruno Mars?"

He looked at me as if I were from Mars. "No," he said, finishing up the cocktails. "Older."

"Like from the nineteen hundreds?"

"Yeah," he said, clearly not impressed by my taste in music. "Try searching 'Big Band.'"

I punched in the search and it came up with a few different stations. "Like this?" I said, playing a song titled 'Moonlight Serenade'.

"That's it."

It was definitely old. Older than old. You could hear the sparks from the vinyl record player. And the sound was dull and organic like real instruments. William brought the drinks over, put them down on the counter and took my hand and we started to dance as if we were my grandparents.

It was slow and soft and tender and I would never have imagined dancing with a man like this before, much less enjoying it. But I was a completely different person that night. I had become a different person in the short time that I had known William.

He held me close and we swayed in the still air of my dimly lit condo. Then he spun me a couple of times as if we were on Dancing with the Stars. When the song ended, he dipped me, looked deeply in my eyes, and kissed me. If I wasn't absolute mush in his arms before, I definitely was now.

He lifted me back up, but kept me close. With my body so close to his and the fabric of my dress so thin, it felt as if we were lying in bed naked.

"You don't have to seduce me, you know," I said through choppy breaths.

"Oh no?"

I shook my head. "Nope. I'll do anything you want."

At this, he took in a tremendous breath as if to account for all that was at stake. "Be careful, Miss Hart," he said, kissing my cheek. "The way you look tonight, I might have to take you up on that offer."

My eyes flared open and I smiled at the thought. "Are you saying what I think you're saying?"

He kissed the side of my eye, then right in front of my ear, making me giggle. "It depends," he said.

"On what?"

More kisses. "On what you think I'm saying."

"Oh yes," I said. "What I think you're saying . . . ."

More kisses. "Yes?"

I put my lips on his ear and softly said, "I think you're willing to change your policy on waiting for marriage."

As I said it, a surge of blood rushed through my torso, causing my back to straighten and push my chest against his.

"Is that what you're saying?" I asked, pleading really.

"Nope," he said, smiling. "I'm saying you just might be the one I'm waiting for."

It took a second to break out of my sensual fog, but when I realized what he was saying I leaned back to look at him in disbelief. Was he saying that he would marry me? The way he confidently kept his gaze on me told me yes.

I was dizzy with the thought. In the moment, when all I could feel was his strong embrace, and his solid frame, and all of the sweet things he'd done, being his bride would have been the most natural thing I could do. But that was all a dream. A mask.

I thought of why I was even there in his arms, in the fancy condo, in the middle of all this political intrigue. I thought about the ledger and the senator's corrupt financing scheme and how I was the only person who could stop it. I thought about my duty as an American and how I couldn't let some feelings get in the way of that.

Of course, as I was telling myself that, I heard it with a sarcastic tone because if I were honest I didn't really believe it any more. Could this powerful man, holding me so gently, treating me with such respect, could he really be behind that corruption? Or had I been misreading him all along? Could it be that it was just a misunderstanding and William was right after all? It certainly seemed that way to me at that moment. The irony was that I had worn the mask so I could conquer the Republicans. Instead, it seemed, it was me who was conquered.

William hummed along with the big band song playing and we started to sway again, carrying on the conversation with just our eyes. If only my eyes could tell him everything that I was thinking. But, no, I had to confess it all—the lies, the condo, the ledger, everything.

When the song ended, we continued swaying anyway. And then I paused. "Come," I said, and led him to the balcony.

* * *

"Wow," he exclaimed as he stepped out onto the deck overlooking the river and the National Mall in the distance. "Your condo is a national treasure."

I leaned back against the rail, ignoring the view and paying attention only to William and his child-like awe.

"You've been hiding this view from me all this time?" he teased.

"That's not all," I said.

"What?" he said, turning toward me. "Do you have a special observatory on the roof or something?"

I shook my head with a smile.

"A water slide into the Potomac?"

"No," I said with a giggle.

"I can only imagine what surprises this young lady has in store for me."

"Do you want to know?"

He just smiled and raised an eyebrow.

"What if it turns your world upside down?" I pressed, the question more for me than for him.

"Especially then," he whispered, and the conviction in his voice sent a pang through my chest. Little did he know that I was the chaos in his meticulously ordered world, and yet here he was, asking for more.

"Even if I have secrets?" My voice was barely audible, the confession on the tip of my tongue.

"Everyone has secrets," he said, brushing a strand of hair from my face. "It's whether you let them define you that matters."

I laughed then, a genuine laugh tinged with sadness, because, right there and then, I knew that no matter how much I wanted this—wanted him—I was on the brink of shattering the very thing that was bringing me back to life.

"Okay. Masks off?" I said, my breath hitching as his gaze locked onto mine.

"Masks off."

"William," I started, my fingers tracing the condensation on the rail. "There's something you should know."

He leaned back against the rail as well, an easy smile playing on his lips. "Let me guess, you're not a fan of my new-fashioned cocktail?"

"No, it's not that," I said with more force than intended. "The truth is . . . I'm not a Republican."

His laughter startled me. It was a rich, warm sound that echoed across the river.

"No, I'm serious," I said, "I lied to you when I said I was a Republican, and I've been lying to you all this time."

"Elizabeth," he said, easing me out of a flurry that I had suddenly gotten into with his characteristic debonair.

"Yes?"

"I knew you weren't a Republican from that first night that we met."

"What?! How is that possible?"

"What Republican that you know of wants to talk about the arts at a bar?"

I cocked my head and made a stupid face. "Okaaayy," I said, "so you've known all along?"

"Well, I've figured as much. Especially because you have always challenged every traditionalist thing or policy measure that I've brought up."

"Heh," I said, thinking back on all of our conversations. "You did seem eager to debate."

"There's nothing more thrilling than to disagree with a beautiful woman."

"Oh!" I chirped, half indignant and half ecstatic at his suave chauvinism.

"No, I was pretty certain that you were a flaming liberal from the start."

"Well, why did you come up and talk to me?" I said, pounding my fist onto his chest.

"Because you're beautiful."

"You said that you wouldn't talk to someone who wasn't a Republican."

"No, I never said that," he said with a grin so shiny it could have swayed a vote. "I said hypothetically that it would present a difficult situation if I did."

I pounded his chest again as if to play fight, and he simply scooped me up with his arms and brought me closer.

"I can't believe you!" I said, pretending to want to break free from his grasp. "All this time—you lied to me!"

"No! You're the one that lied," he said, laughing. "I just played along."

"Ugh!" I grunted, knowing that he had me. "So you lied implicitly."

"Well, you lied explicitly. Which is worse?"

"Ugh, and you made me act like I support the flat tax and Barry George and . . . and . . . old music!"

"Be honest—you liked dancing to that song."

It took me a second but I finally admitted it. "Yes," I said, "I loved it. And I love you opening doors for me and pulling out my seat and your tuxedo and . . . ." I started caressing his neck and kissing him. "I love everything about you."

"Even the flat tax?"

"Even the flat tax!"

"Really?"

"I mean, the way you describe it is right on. I was so blind before I met you."

We kissed and caressed and caressed and kissed. And then I pushed myself back and hit him on the chest again. "It's not fair!"

"What?" he said, laughing.

"You can't play with my heart like that," I said, mad at him, but I was really talking to myself.

"Here's a thought," he said, his voice calming me down from my ledge. "Maybe you've secretly been a Republican all along and were only looking for an excuse to be one in the open."

"No, that's not it," I said. "I don't think that's it."

"No?"

"No," I said, pushing back again. "There's more."

He raised an eyebrow. "More secrets?"

I nodded. "Mmmhm."

"Don't tell me, you're actually a trapeze monkey for a traveling circus?"

I was so lost in thought that his joke didn't even register. "It's worse."

"I don't know what could be worse than that."

"Okay," I said, sucking in a huge breath. I looked up to him as if it were the last time.

"What is it?"

"This . . . condo . . . isn't mine," I started.

He let his gaze bounce around our surroundings.

"The BMW, this dress, none of this is mine."

"Okaaayy."

"It was all given to me by Vanessa Martinez and the Kenton Peats campaign under the presumption that I would use it to get close to you."

I could see the thoughts ricocheting around his brain as he tried to make sense of what I was saying.

"I was told to date you in hopes that I could dig up some dirt on Barry George."

"The Caron financing?"

"Yes," I said, solemn.

"You are spying on me?"

I closed my eyes when I heard it and nodded.

"Hhmm. But, Elizabeth," he said, "why are you telling me this?"

"Because I don't want to hurt you," I said. "I . . . I . . . ."

I didn't quite know if I wanted to apologize or give an explanation. What came out was the truest thing that I had ever said.

"I love you."

Once I said it, I scrunched my face, knowing that I shouldn't have introduced such a huge thing in the middle of all of these other huge things. But, it was true and the only thing that mattered at that moment. "I love you, and I don't want you to be hurt by this."

He was still puzzling through everything when I reopened my eyes. "Well this is something else entirely," he said. I could tell something was different because for the first time he appeared stunned, like I had gotten through his confident veneer.

"I guess I'm either the world's worst spy or the world's best romantic."

"You have a convincing case for both," he said. He allowed a smile, which I took to be a good sign.

"Somewhere along the way, it stopped being an act."

"I'm glad that it did."

I scanned his lapel as if to find the answer in its fine Italian threads.

"Listen, I know that you're going to hate me," I said. "You probably want to stomp out of here and forget that I ever existed."

He clicked his teeth as if to confirm my suspicion.

"All I ask of you is to know that, even though I did this, I did learn, and I grew to become a better person because of you. Don't hate me because of it."

"Oh," he said, lifting his head toward the sky and smiling. "I don't think I can hate you."

"You can't?"

"Look, I know you were pretending to be someone else, and I am not really sure who that someone else is supposed to be, but something tells me I know really well who the real Elizabeth Hart is. Libby Hart from Indiana. Libby Hart who is very passionate about helping people. That's the girl I know."

I almost started to cry as he rehearsed my life.

"And if you ask me, she's quite a wonderful young lady," he said. "She just got caught up in the rat race is all."

"Well, for the record," I said, laughing, "you might know the real me better than I know myself."

He lifted my head so he could look in my eyes. I resisted at first, but complied.

"So does that mean you don't hate me?"

"I don't hate you," he said.

"You're not going to throw me to into the Potomac?"

He shook his head.

"Does this mean we can have sex?" I joked.

"Uh, the answer to that is still 'No'."

I placed my hand on his chest and rested my head on my hand. It was the coziest place I could imagine being and, after I feared I had lost it, there it was.

"Now what?" he prompted.

I leaned back to look him in the eyes. "They expect me to give them the ledger," I said and he lit up as if to deny it. "But I am not going to do it," I said, cutting him off.

"They know you have it?"

"Yes," I said, sullen. "I could say the file is corrupted or something."

"They're not going to believe it."

"That's fine," I said. "They can deal. I'm going to go in tomorrow and quit."

"Really? You're going to give all of this up?" he said, rolling his head around as if to show off the condo.

"They're going to throw me out of here one way or another. I can't let that dictate my answer."

"True."

"No," I said, stern. "They are the lie now. And I can't go on living a lie. This is the truth." I patted his chest.

"You're a brave girl," he said, and I embraced him.

Standing there in his arms I felt as if I could have spent the rest of my life without moving an inch. Part of me wanted to stay closed off from the rest of the world, from Vanessa, from the campaign, from everything. But I knew that I would have to face it all. At least, it seemed, I would have William Benjamin by my side in doing it.

"Are you sure you don't hate me?" I asked, my voice fluttering like a moth.

"I'm sure," he said without hesitation.

"I have a feeling we won't run out of things to argue about, at least."

"Never," he agreed, his laughter mingling with mine, sealing an unspoken pact of affection amid the chaos of our colliding worlds.

CHAPTER 19

I PUSHED OPEN the door to the campaign office, my heart thumping in protest. This was mutiny, my inner voice growled, but I had already branded myself a rebel with every ignored text and the ledger still clutched in my metaphorical fist.

"Libby?!" Gabby's voice pierced the charged silence like a siren. Heads turned, eyes widened. "What are you doing here? You'll get discovered."

"It doesn't matter," I said, stomping toward Vanessa's office. "It's over."

"What's over?" Gabby said, pulling me to the side. "Libby, come tell me what's going on."

"The spying, the lying, everything," I said. "I can't continue to live like this."

"Keep it down," Gabby hissed, glancing around nervously. "We don't need Vanessa catching wind of this before we could—"

"Before we could what, Gabby?" I cut her off, the words tumbling out faster than I could reel them back. "Hide? Skulk around corners?"

Gabby's eyes were wide, imploring. "Libby, please. This isn't you."

"That's where you're wrong, Gabby," I challenged, the fight in me igniting. I was tired of being a pawn, tired of playing games. "This is exactly who I am. It's taken me all of this game playing to finally figure that out."

Her brow furrowed, confusion mingled with concern. "What happened?"

"It's William," I said, putting down my guard to finally connect with my friend. "I love him, and I can't do this to him."

"You . . . what?" Gabby stammered, her disbelief tangible.

"Love. Him." I punctuated each word, feeling the weight of them settle between us.

"Libby, he is a Republican!" Gabby blurted out as if that explained everything, as if love had party lines.

"Thanks for the memo," I retorted, my lips twitching despite the gravity of the situation. "I hadn't noticed."

"Libby, think about what you were saying. Your job, your career . . . " Gabby trailed off, the unsaid words lingering like specters.

"Sometimes, Gabs, you have to follow your heart, even if it means crossing the aisle." I squared my shoulders, ready to face the firing squad of consequences.

"Even if it means quitting?" She was grasping at straws now, trying to tether me to the familiar.

"Especially then," I said, my resolve steeling. "I have to do this."

"Are you sure?" Gabby's eyes searched mine, looking for the hesitation, the doubt. But there was none to be found.

"As sure as I am that Vanessa wears shoulder pads to intimidate us," I replied, a wry smile tugging at my lips.

"Listen, Hart, I have always had your back," Gabby exhaled, resignation settling over her features like a blanket. "But I can't support you on this one."

"I know Gabby, I am going to do this on my own," I promised, feeling the edges of my world tilting. But it was okay. For once, I was the one doing the spinning.

* * *

"Libby Hart, in my office. Now!" Vanessa's voice cut through the campaign chaos like a scythe, and every pair of eyes followed me as I marched toward the lioness' den.

I rapped lightly on the open door—more out of courtesy than necessity—and stepped into the sleek, modern cave that was Vanessa Martinez's lair. The walls adorned with political memorabilia seemed to close in on me, and her brown eyes zeroed in like guided missiles.

"I expected you to send that ledger last night," she said.

"Vanessa," I began, my heart thrumming in my chest, "I can't give you the ledger."

"Excuse me?" Her voice was deceptively calm, her eyes narrowing into slits.

"Politics shouldn't be about winning at all costs. It's about doing what's right," I said, feeling a strange sense of liberation with each word.

Vanessa leaned back in her chair, steepling her fingers.

"Libby, dear, naivety is a dress that has never been in fashion in D.C." She shook her head, her sleek hair unmoving, as if lacquered into place.

"Then I clearly don't belong," I shot back, pulling my keys from my pocket and placing them on her desk with a decisive clink. "You can have your condo and your BMW back. I quit."

Her sharp inhale was the only sign of surprise before she regained her composure. "You can't just quit, you know. You signed a contract to work for us, and we expect you to fulfill that contract."

"Things change," I said, "I can no longer fulfill my duty."

"Well, we're just going to have to see what our lawyers say about that," she said, waving to the door.

One of the black suit lawyers from the other day poked his head in. "We've got it."

"Thank you," Vanessa said.

And the lawyer left.

I watched as Vanessa very happily turned to her desk work. "That is all," she said.

My face grew contorted as I tried to figure out what was going on.

"What was that?" I inquired.

"That is all, you are dismissed," she said, gleeful as can be.

"Dismissed?" I stormed. "What did that lawyer say he had?"

Vanessa looked at me with a smile so artificial it could have peeled off her face. "Oh Libby, you are precious, aren't you?"

"What did he get, Vanessa?"

"You think that you can come in here and boss me around?"

I picked up my phone, and glanced at the screen. "What did he get?"

"The ledger, of course," she said, plain as the day.

"How did you . . . ?" I looked at my phone again, trying to figure out how they swiped the file.

"Oh honey you don't think that I would put you up in a fancy Georgetown condo and BMW and not get what I was after, do you?"

"I did not give you authorization to take that!"

"Do you think that really matters?" she said. "We've got the lawyers, we've got the tech team, we've got the DOJ. We can do as we please."

"That's not right!"

She actually paused and thought about it. "No, you're right. It's not right. But, sweetheart, it's like I keep telling you, sometimes you have to embrace the lesser evil for the greater good," she explained, her tone patronizing beyond belief.

"Is that what we are now? Evil?" I demanded, my anger rising like mercury on a hot day.

"Only as evil as necessary," she replied coolly. "Now, if you'll excuse me, I have a campaign to win."

I stared at her, feeling the sting of betrayal from someone I once admired. My hands balled into fists at my sides. "I hope it's worth it, Vanessa. I really do." My words were edged with ice, but they didn't seem to pierce her armor.

"Politics is a game, Libby. And I play to win." Vanessa's final statement hung in the air.

"Well, I'm playing for the other team, then," I said, causing

Vanessa to laugh.

"Do what you have to do," she said, looking at her watch. "In about an hour, Kenton Peats is going on an interview to expose Barry George, and that other team of yours is going to be no more."

As I was hearing her words, it was as if the air was sucked out of the room. I suddenly felt like I was suffocating. "You can't do that."

"Oh no?" she said. "We just did."

I turned sharply, striding out of her office with a mixture of fury and defeat. William's face flashed in my mind, his bright eyes, his gentle smile—a stark contrast to the duplicity I'd just witnessed. I had to make things right, somehow.

The campaign office buzzed around me, but I was in my own silent storm. I pushed through the door, leaving behind a life I could no longer live. It was time to start playing by a new set of rules—my own.

* * *

I fumbled with my phone, the sleek device slipping against the sheen of sweat on my palms. My thumb hovered over William's contact—his name a beacon of hope in the chaos that had become my life. I pressed 'Call' and brought the phone to my ear, each ring echoing like a gavel in the courtroom of my anxiety.

"Come on, William . . . please," I muttered under my breath, pacing the narrow alley beside the office building where I could still see the shadows of staffers moving behind tinted windows.

The call went to voicemail, his cheerful greeting twisting the knife of dread lodged in my gut. "Hey, it's Will. I'm probably out saving the republic or something equally heroic. Leave a message!"

"William, it's me," I began, desperation seeping into my voice. "Listen, things have gone nuclear here, and—"

A beep cut me off. Out of time or out of luck—I wasn't sure which was worse. With a growl of frustration, I pocketed my phone, the weight of my decision bearing down on me.

"Okay, Libby Hart," I whispered to myself, "time to channel your inner action hero."

I searched for the George campaign office and saw that it was just a few blocks away. If I couldn't stop them from blasting the ledger across the media, at least I could warn them that it was going to happen so they could do something about it.

I set off at a brisk walk, my mind whirling with plans and counterplans. The heels of my boots clacked against the concrete with military precision as I dodged pedestrians, my internal monologue running like a ticker tape of turmoil.

"Girlfriend ditches campaign, loses company car, possibly boyfriend—all before lunchtime. Film at eleven," I jested silently, the humor a flimsy shield against the barrage of emotions threatening to spill over.

As I navigated the labyrinth of D.C.'s streets, landmarks passing by in a blur, I could almost hear the sitcom laugh track underscoring my dramatic exit. But there was nothing funny about the burning bridges in my rear view mirror—or the uncertainty of the path ahead.

"Excuse me!" A man in a suit narrowly avoided a collision with my shoulder. "Watch where you're going!"

"Sorry!" I called back, not slowing my stride. "Political emergency! You know how it is!"

My determination morphed into resolve with each step. I had to find William.

CHAPTER 20

I BARRELED THROUGH the door of the George campaign office like a hurricane named 'Basa Basa'. "I need to see William!" My voice sliced through the cacophony of phone calls and clacking keyboards, but it might as well have been a whisper for all the attention it garnered. The staffers were engrossed in their own political bubble, immune to my growing panic.

"Does anyone care that Kenton Peats is about to drop a bombshell on the George campaign?!" I yelled, my frustration boiling over.

Heads finally turned, eyes wide as if they had just noticed a live wire in their midst.

A staffer, his tie askew and forehead shining with the sheen of campaign stress, scurried away, probably to fetch someone— anyone—to deal with the madwoman disrupting their orchestrated chaos.

Moments later, Simon Katz appeared before me, his sandy blonde hair seeming to bristle with curiosity. "Miss Hart, to what do we owe the pleasure?" His voice dripping with sarcasm that grated on my already frayed nerves.

"I need to see William, now." My foot tapped an impatient staccato on the tiled floor.

"Will is at a campaign event," Simon informed me with maddening nonchalance, scratching at his jaw. "He can't exactly step out to chat."

"Ugh," I fumed, incredulous. "I really need to talk with him. This could change everything!"

"Sorry, Elizabeth," he said, though his tone suggested anything but. "You know how these events are. No cell phones, full attention on the deep pockets in the room."

My heart sank even as my mind raced, trying to map out where William might be.

I pictured him, charming and composed, working the room with ease. If only I could have channeled some of that charm to get past Simon's blockade.

"Listen, Kenton Peats is going to leak the ledger you sent me on an interview in less than an hour."

"Oh is he?" He said, incredulous.

"I really need to talk with William—can you get him on the phone?" I pleaded.

"How did Kenton Peats get ahold of the ledger?" he inquired smarmily.

"Well, Vanessa stole it right off my phone," I blurted out, chest still heaving from the mad dash across town. "Kenton Peats is going to detonate that bombshell in less than an hour."

Simon's eyebrows arch, a revelation lighting his mischievous eyes. "Vanessa? Martinez?"

"Yes, Vanessa Martinez with the Peats campaign."

"Oh, she's a shark all right. Figures she'd pull something like this."

"Shark is one word for her," I said, rolling my eyes. "But we've got bigger fish to fry right now."

"So . . . ," Simon interjected, leaning against a desk littered with campaign paraphernalia. "How did Vanessa Martinez nab the file?"

"They stole it while I was at the Peats campaign office!"

"Well, what were you doing at the Peats HQ, Miss Hart?"

"Doesn't matter," I replied tersely, not liking the way he said my name as if it's some sort of punchline. "All that matters now is that William needs to know about this, and you're going to tell me where he is."

"Slow down, detective." Simon said, folding his arms, clearly enjoying my discomfort. "I think it matters very much indeed. Why were you at the Peats campaign?"

"Listen, I was a part of the campaign once. But I'm not any more."

"Once?"

"Yeah, once."

"When?"

"Like, well," I stuttered. "William knows all about this, so it doesn't help to go over it with you, what we need to do is to make sure we have damage control after Peats drops the bomb."

"How do I know you're not playing some double agent game here?"

"Uugghhh! Because I'm standing here telling you what happened!" I threw my hands up, exasperation distorting my voice into a yell.

"Sorry, sweetheart. 'Trust but verify' and all that jazz," he said, but his tone was more like he was eating popcorn while watching my meltdown.

"Sweetheart?" I snorted, my patience fraying like a worn-out flag. "You might want to update your sexism software, Katz. It's about four decades out of date."

"Touché," he conceded with a chuckle. "But I still can't give you Will's location."

"Can't or won't?" I challenged, stepping closer, trying to will the information out of him through sheer proximity.

"Pick your poison."

"Fine." My jaw clenched tighter than a vice grip. "Keep your secrets. I'll find William without your help."

"Good luck with that," Simon called after me, a smirk plastered on his lips.

At that moment I felt a buzz on my phone. It was William. I held it up and flashed it at Simon as if I had just won a bet.

"No such thing as luck in politics, Simon," I retorted without turning back, pushing through the door and out onto the sidewalk.

"William!" I said, his name like a buoy in a tempest.

"Elizabeth Hart," he said, jovial. "I got your message. Is everything—"

"There isn't time," I said, cutting him off. "Where are you?"

"Can you get to the InterContinental? We've got a watch party going on."

I looked up as if I could see it down the street. "Yes, I'll be there in five."

We hung up and I dashed off toward the hotel.

CHAPTER 21

I STORMED INTO the InterContinental hotel, my heart racing as if it was trying to outrun my body on a mission. The ballroom swallowed me whole, its walls draped in shadows, save for the glaring light from a big screen where Kenton Peats' face loomed larger than life. The C-SPAN interview projected before the room held dozens of spectators in rapt attention. It was as if they were at a movie premiere, not on the cusp of a political scandal.

"William!" I called out, my voice lost in the sea of political chatter and the blaring broadcast. My eyes darted from one cluster of people to another, searching for that familiar head of hair, that cocky stance. Nothing. William was nowhere to be found, and, with every passing second, my desperation ticked up a notch.

"Oh, you're Elizabeth Hart, right?" A young staffer, all grin and no clue, materialized beside me. He looked as though he had dressed in the dark, his tie a skewed homage to patriotism.

"Where's William?" I snapped, not in the mood for pleasantries. "It's urgent."

"William's tied up at the moment," he said with an ease that grated on my nerves. He gestured toward the bar, as if a drink could fix the incoming disaster. "Why don't you grab a seat? Watch the show."

I fixed him with a glare that could curdle milk. "We don't have time," I hissed, pointing to the image of Peats, who looked about as trustworthy as a used car salesman at that moment. "He's going to leak the ledger."

"Isn't it awesome?" the staffer enthused, clearly missing the gravity of the situation. "We've all been waiting for this to play out."

'Awesome' wasn't the word I'd have chosen. 'Cataclysmic', maybe. But his reaction was off-script—like he was in on a joke that I was the punchline to. I clenched my fists, resisting the urge to shake some sense into him. Instead, I turned on my heel, determined to find William myself, but my feet rooted to the spot as the gravity of what was unfolding on-screen hit me.

I slumped onto a bar stool, the leather creaking under the sudden burden of my spiraling thoughts. The bartender offered me a sympathetic nod and slid over a glass of water—no ice, no lemon, just plain and unassuming like my mood. I clutched it, feeling the coolness seep into my palms as Kenton Peats filled the screen with his grandstanding.

"Barry George's campaign," Peats declared with a flourish that bordered on theatrical, "has been luxuriously funded by none other than Didier Caron." He paused for effect, letting the name hang heavy in the air—a name synonymous with scandal and extremism.

My breath hitched, heart pounding against my ribs like a

drum line in overdrive. This was it—the disaster I'd feared. Peats lifted a print out of the ledger, waving it like a flag of victory. "And here we have the proof," he said, the smugness in his tone making my skin crawl. "This ledger belongs to Barry George's campaign."

Around me, a ripple of excitement surged through the crowd. They were leaning forward, eyes wide, as if they were watching the season finale of their favorite political thriller. It was bizarre—like attending a surprise party for a funeral.

"A fine denouement," I muttered, my voice tinged with the anxiety blooming in my stomach. I nervously took a sip of someone else's abandoned beer, the bitterness of the hops mirroring my mood.

The interview continued to unfold, and I found myself holding my breath, bracing for the impact of whatever shock wave was about to ripple through the crowd. In this city, scandal was currency, and Peats was either making a fortune or going bankrupt before our very eyes.

"Mister Peats, this is quite the allegation," the journalist interjected, her voice razor-sharp with skepticism. "But there seem to be some irregularities with your evidence."

Peats' confident smirk wavered.

"Could you explain why these entries," she continued, her finger tracing lines on a copy of the ledger, "appear to be more closely associated with your own campaign?"

The room erupted. Excitement morphed into an electric frenzy, a buzz that felt more like vindication than shock. I squinted at the faces around me, reading their expressions like subtitles to a foreign film. Were they actually cheering this on?

"Must be a mistake," Peats stammered, his composure cracking like thin ice beneath heavy boots.

"Or perhaps a deliberate misdirection?" the journalist prodded, relentless.

A sarcastic gasp rose from the spectators, and I found myself caught in the undertow of disbelief. Was this really happening?

"Deliberate?" Peats echoed, his voice now a fragile thread about to snap.

"Indeed, an intriguing turn of events, Mister Peats," the journalist concluded with a knowing look, one eyebrow arched in triumph.

I sat, rooted to the stool, mind racing faster than a scandal on social media. If this was a disaster, why did it feel like everyone else had read the script but me?

* * *

The journalist's finger paused over a name that sent a chill down my spine. "And what about this entry, Mister Peats? A donation from an individual recently indicted for money laundering?"

Peats' face drained of color, his lips quivering as if he was about to engage in a tango with the truth and found himself sorely out of step. "That . . . that's preposterous," he sputtered, but the conviction had left his voice. It was like watching a balloon deflate, sad and slow.

"Is it?" The journalist's tone was silk over steel, and I couldn't help but admire her, even as I felt my world start to crumble.

"Absolutely," Peats insisted, but his eyes darted around, seeking an exit.

"Because there's more," she went on, her words slicing through the tension like a machete through underbrush. "Several more names here are linked to your own campaign rather than George's."

A bead of sweat traveled down Peats' temple, a lonely river charting new territory. He stood abruptly, his chair screeching across the floor like a scream in a silent movie.

"Um, maybe we have to . . . ," Peats said, and then turned to the camera before jumping out of his seat and running off.

A clip of Barney flashed on the screen as the interview cut away.

As Peats fled the scene, the crowd in the ballroom exploded with cheers and laughter and applause. Whooping as if their favorite quarterback had just thrown a Hail Mary pass straight into the end zone. I sat there, my heart pounding a rhythm of betrayal, as the realization washed over me: I was the only one not in on the joke.

Before I could digest the spectacle, the screen flickered off, and William took the stage, his grin a mile wide. Microphone in hand, he looked every bit the maestro ready to lead his orchestra.

"All right, what a show!" he boomed, and the room obliged with enthusiasm that should've been reserved for New Year's Eve. "We've got miles to go before we sleep, but tonight, I think we can celebrate that there won't be a Senator Kenton Peats any time soon!"

They whistled and clapped, some even high-fiving as if they'd all collectively scored a winning goal. My chest tightened, each cheer a hammer blow to my conscience.

"Pollsters are already buzzing," William continued, the glint in his eye that of a man who'd just pulled off a magic trick. "We're looking at a five to ten point drop for Peats in the coming weeks."

I blinked back a sting of tears, not from sadness, but from sheer, unadulterated fury. This was the 'big one' alright. The big lie. The big game. And unbeknown to me, I was the pivotal player.

Clutching the edge of the bar, I steadied myself against the tide of deception. This wasn't politics; it was theater, and I'd been cast as the unwitting fool. Well, bravo, I wanted to say. Bravo for the performance of a lifetime.

* * *

I swiveled on my heel, the cacophony of the bar fading into a dull murmur as I faced the living embodiment of smugness. There stood Simon Katz, his sandy hair tousled perfectly, a wolfish grin spread across his face.

"Simon," I exhaled his name like a curse. "What in the world is going on?"

"Libby, Libby, Libby," he tsked, shaking his head with feigned disappointment. "Did your Kenton Peats leak the ledger?"

"He's not my Kenton Peats," I asserted, but then I realized what had happened. "It was a set up, wasn't it?"

"Hmm? Oh the ledger? Uh huh," Simon said, creepy as ever.

"More like a trap. When slinging mud, you often get it on your face."

My heart thumped against my ribcage. "A trap?" The word tasted bitter on my tongue.

"Indeed." He leaned closer, his breath smelling faintly of mint and mischief. "That ledger I sent you? You might have thought it incriminated Barry George. But in reality it was Kenton Peats' own financial ledger."

My eyes bulged out of their sockets. "How in the world?"

"You thought it would light up George's campaign, but, in reality, it was meant to light up Peats' campaign like a bonfire. And, oh, did it blaze."

The revelation sucker-punched the air from my lungs. "You're saying you fabricated evidence that would burn your own candidate so that Peats would leak it and have it backfire?" I struggled to connect the dots as twisted as they were.

"Oh, fabricated is such an ugly word." He winked. "Let's just say we set the stage for a performance, and you and Martinez and Peats danced right onto it."

"Damn it, Simon," I spat, anger flaring. "Did you know? About me working for the Democrats?"

His smirk widened, confirming my worst fears before the words left his lips. "Of course, we knew. You think Will just stumbled into your life by pure chance?"

The revelation hit me with the force of a sucker punch. Betrayal burned through my veins, igniting a fury that threatened to overflow. Before I could unleash a verbal tirade, William bounded over, radiant as a groom seeing his bride on their wedding day.

"Well, Elizabeth, we pulled it off!" His eyes sparkled with triumph, and I wanted to smash something beautiful – preferably one of those crystal champagne flutes being hoisted by an overly enthusiastic staffer.

"Used me is what you did," I said through gritted teeth, my hands balled into fists. "Played me for a fool while preaching about integrity!"

"Come on, Elizabeth," William said, feigning innocence so poorly it could have been slapstick. "You said yourself you were switching teams. This was all part of the game."

"Game?" My voice was a loaded gun, cocked and ready to fire. "What happened to honesty and integrity, William? Was that just another pawn in your political chess match?"

"I still think your integrity strategy is genius," he replied, unfazed. "And yes, I think we should still use it—"

"Strategy?!" The word was a hiss, venomous and sharp. "Integrity isn't a strategy, William, that's the whole point!"

"Don't be dramatic—" Simon started, but I was already turning away.

"Save it, lemur boy," I spat out, every muscle in my body coiled tight as I pushed through the crowd. They were oblivious, wrapped up in their victory, their laughter grating against my eardrums.

I burst out of the ballroom, the sound of my boots hitting the marble floor echoed the rapid pounding of my heart. I didn't stop. Couldn't stop. Out the door, I started to run. Away. Anywhere. It didn't matter. I just had to run.

CHAPTER 22

I WAS PERCHED on the cool marble of the Lincoln Memorial stairs, lost in a sea of turmoil, my gaze fixed on the Reflecting Pool as if it could somehow mirror back a solution to the chaos my life had become. The weight of betrayal and deceit heavy on my shoulders, punctuated by the occasional tourist snapping pictures blissfully unaware of the political drama at their feet.

"I thought I might find you here," a familiar voice cut through my mental fog, laced with concern. I didn't have to look up to see it was Gabby, taking a seat beside me and joining me in my existentialist glare.

"Hey," I managed, my voice a whisper that seemed too small for the grandeur around us.

"Vanessa is out," she reported.

The news was not shocking. Nothing was at this point.

"It looks like Peats is pretty much done for, and George will run away in this race."

"Ugh," I said.

"Talk about a turn of events."

"We got played so bad."

Gabby's sigh was emblematic of our shared dismay. "Sucks," she said.

"You were right, Gabby," I let out. "It is a mean town. The meanest town there is."

"You have to know, Libby," she said, "I had nothing to do with it."

"Yeah," I said, almost numb to the thought that my best friend might have been a part of the scheme.

But then the dam broke. Words were unnecessary as tears spilled down my cheeks, each one carrying the weight of disappointment and suspicion. I leaned into Gabby's embrace, letting her warmth seep into the cold places doubt had chilled inside me.

"Everything . . . it was all a setup, Gabby," I sobbed into her shoulder, my voice muffled by her soft cardigan. "I don't know who I can trust anymore. Hell, I'm not even sure I can trust myself."

"I know, I know," she soothed, rubbing my back in slow circles. "It's such a dirty game, Lib. If you're not getting hurt, you're the one dishing out the pain."

"I know. And that's the worst part," I said, unbelieving. "I knew that that's the way this town worked and I still got involved."

"Ugh," Gabby replied. "I'm sorry I dragged you into this fray, Libs. Really, I am."

"You don't have to apologize," I said, pulling back slightly to wipe away the last remnants of my tear-streaked campaign strategy.

I stood up as if to get a better vantage on the National Mall before me. "Oh! Remember when we thought there were good guys in this town?" I mused, wrapping my arms around my torso. "The silver knight riding in on his policy papers to save the day?"

"Silver knights turn into gray bureaucrats so fast in this city," Gabby sighed. "Maybe they start off shiny, but the swamp dirties them in an instant."

I chuckled despite myself, a wry sound that echoed off Lincoln's stony gaze. "What does that make us then? The damsels who forgot to distress?"

"More like the jesters who took a wrong turn and ended up in a tragedy instead of a comedy." Gabby's lips twisted up at the corners as she said it, and her humor was infectious.

"Or maybe we're the fools for thinking we could ever change the script." My laughter bubbled up again, this time a little louder, a little less tinged with cynicism.

"Hey, don't knock it. Fools are the only ones who get to speak truth to power without losing their heads." Gabby nudged me with her elbow, prodding a smile onto my face.

"True," I conceded, "but it's usually because no one takes them seriously enough to bother with the guillotine."

"Technicalities, Libby, technicalities." She grinned, standing and brushing off her pants. "Your carriage awaits, m'lady." Gabby gestured grandly toward the street where her Prius was parked. "Though, it's less 'pumpkin' and more 'economical hatchback.'"

"Charming," I said, following her down the steps, each one feeling lighter than the last. "But I think this damsel is about done with the kingdom of D.C."

Gabby paused, turning to look at me with a mix of concern

and understanding. "You're serious?"

"Dead serious." I shrugged, trying to seem nonchalant, but the weight of the decision settled on my shoulders like a mantle. "This place . . . it changes people. And not for the better."

"Libby Hart, conceding the match?" Gabby raised an eyebrow, a playful challenge in her tone.

"More like withdrawing from the tournament." I met her gaze squarely. "I've realized that not fitting into this environment might just be the sanest thing about me."

She batted the idea around in her head. "I loved having you here," she said. "It felt right to have my best friend out here with me."

"I know," I said. "It was the best. But I need to be back home."

I could feel her assessing my broken-down stance. I was beaten, and she knew it.

"Then let's get you home, then, away from the madness." She looped an arm through mine, her solidarity as tangible as the resolve solidifying in my chest.

"Home," I echoed, allowing a genuine smile to form. "That sounds exactly right."

CHAPTER 23

THE LAST OF the cardboard boxes sat half-closed, like clamshells unsure if they wanted to keep their pearls or join the sea of my past. I patrolled the room one final time, my hands ghosting over surfaces that had once been mine. With a sigh heavier than the packed books, I flicked on the TV, granting myself one last voyeuristic glimpse at the D.C. circus.

"Barry George is steamrolling ahead," intoned the silver-haired anchor, his voice as smooth and cold as a well-used shovel. My gaze skated over the screen where the presidential race was being dissected like a frog in a high school lab.

"Fourteen percent lead since Peats' spectacular nosedive," chimed in another commentator, her lipstick as red as the deficit numbers she delighted in. "Frankly, I think we can stick a fork in this race. It's done."

"Done and dusted," I murmured, sealing the tape on my life here with more conviction.

"Wait," cut in a lone wolf among the sheep, his tie rebelliously askew. "There's a wild card yet to be played." He leaned forward, his eyes glinting like he was sharing Washington's best-kept secret. "What about integrity? That's what the voters crave now, a phoenix rising from the ashes of scandal."

"Integrity?" The panel scoffed in unison, a practiced chorus of cynics.

"Where will they find it? Not with Peats or George," the maverick pressed on, unfazed.

"Charlie Archer," he ventured, throwing the name into the ring like a grenade. "If he runs as an independent, mark my words, he'll vacuum up Peats' votes and suck out a chunk of George's too."

"Archer?" The word tickled my brain, fluttering like a campaign banner in the winds of possibility. But I squashed the butterfly before it could take flight. Wishful thinking.

"Long shot doesn't quite cover it," I said to no one, but the TV seemed to take it personally.

"Never underestimate a dark horse," the commentator warned, wagging a finger as if through the screen and at me. "Politics, love, war—it's all about who throws the best Hail Mary."

"Or who packs the best exit strategy," I shot back, my humor almost as dry as my throat.

"Surely you don't believe this Archer fairy tale?" the red-lipped siren sang, her disbelief dripping with enough sarcasm to corrode iron.

"Stranger things have happened," I conceded, my heart giving a traitorous little skip at the thought.

"Like a political strategist believing in fairy tales?" I chided myself, taping up the last of my optimism with the box marked

'Miscellaneous.'

"Stay tuned," the wolf grinned, "the real show is just starting."

"Show's over for me," I declared, hitting the power button with a definitive click. Politics might be full of comebacks, but I was getting out before any more plot twists.

* * *

The cardboard fortress I'd built around me seemed almost cozy—my own little island of corrugated walls in an ocean of political sharks. Just as I was about to declare myself queen of Castle Box-It-Up, a whirlwind that answered to the name of Gabby Jean burst through my door.

"Libby, you have got to see this!" Gabby trilled, her wild curls bouncing with each exclamation point she spoke.

"Gabby, ever heard of knocking?" I teased, but the urgency in her eyes told me this wasn't just another one of her 'the vending machine is giving out free snacks' moments.

"Read," she thrust the newspaper at me with the drama of a Shakespearean actor with the winning lottery numbers.

"Fine, fine," I said, scanning the headline her finger jabbed at: "George Campaign Shakeup: Top Strategist Resigns."

"William quit his job?" My voice betrayed a note of disbelief mingled with a perverse sort of pride.

"Keep reading," Gabby nudged, her smile spreading like she had just passed Go and collected two hundred dollars.

"' . . . citing his frustration with the unethical culture of D.C. politics . . . '" I read aloud. "Wow, he's really throwing down the gauntlet."

"Check out this part," she pointed again, tapping the paper so fiercely I half expected her finger to bore right through to the other side. "'Someone I met recently showed me what real integrity looks like—it's possible, even here, among the wolves.'"

"Subtle," I muttered, unsure whether to be flattered or skeptical. "He's not talking about me, Gabby."

"Who else, Lib? You're Little Red Riding Hood with a spine of steel." She grinned, her optimism practically blinding. "You should stay. And you know . . . maybe give it another shot with William?"

"Give it a shot? With William?" I scoffed, the thought ricocheting in my brain like a pinball. "That ship has sailed, hit an iceberg, and sunk to the bottom of the Potomac."

"Libby Hart, don't you dare go Titanic on me now," Gabby chided, her hands on her hips in mock indignation.

"Washington's no place for fairy tales," I said, even though a part of me yearned to believe in something more than just political power plays. "Besides, I've already bought my ticket home."

"Return it," Gabby countered. "Stay."

"Gabby, it's not . . . ," I trailed off, the words getting tangled in the web of what-ifs sprouting in my mind.

"Come on, Lib. This is your third-act twist—the part where the heroine realizes she's been running in the wrong direction."

"Running has kept me in shape," I argued weakly, knowing full well how stubborn she could be when she latched onto an idea. "Let's face it, my love life is less rom-com and more cautionary tale."

"Then let's write a new ending," Gabby beamed, all hope and Hollywood sparkle.

"Life isn't scripted, Gabs," I sighed, feeling the weight of every packed box anchor me to reality. But tucked beneath the skepticism was a kernel of curiosity, a tiny voice whispering that maybe, just maybe, the joke was on me for giving up too soon.

* * *

A rhythmic rapping on the door cut through the room like a roll call. "That's gotta be the movers," I threw out, swiping a last look at my stark, nearly empty D.C. apartment. "You can help, right?"

"Help you move? Sure, what else are friends for?" Gabby sighed theatrically as we opened the door to welcome two burly men with shirts on that said 'The Box Brigade'.

"Hey fellas," I greeted the two gruff men whose biceps bulged like they moonlighted as arm wrestling champs. "Everything labeled 'Fragile' is actually filled with my shattered dreams and political aspirations, so I would appreciate it if you handle it with care."

"And anything that has 'Gabby' written in pink is mine—take it straight to my place!" Gabby chimed in, her infectious grin doing little to soften the stoicism of our moving muscle.

"Don't confuse them," I said under my breath.

"All right, let's get this show on the road," I directed, and the men started carting off my life to the truck waiting outside.

Gabby pretended to help by pushing a box here and there,

the least earnest mover in the history of movers.

"That's not helpful, Gabs," I said.

"Hey, I'm not going to do anything to precipitate the demise of my social life and the only thing good left in D.C."

As I was giving her a sarcastic thanks, a clamor erupted from just beyond the open doorway.

"No, no, no, take it back!" a familiar voice bellowed outside, causing me to exchange a bewildered glance with Gabby. We hustled to the source of the commotion to find William, of all people, clutching onto my beloved sofa like a lifeline in stormy seas.

"Seriously?" I huffed, hands planted firmly on my hips. "Ignore him, guys. He's probably just panhandling for donations."

"Elizabeth, listen—" William started, but I cut him off with a wave.

"Keep moving, guys," I instructed the movers, who shrugged and continued their sofa-schlepping mission.

"Wait!" William protested, flashing a wad of cash like a high roller in Vegas. The movers paused, looking between us with raised brows, clearly wondering if they'd stumbled onto a live taping of some absurd reality show. "Put everything back where it was," he insisted.

"Absolutely not." I turned to the movers. "You can keep his donation to the 'Libby Hart Moving Forward Fund,' but the furniture goes in the truck."

William's eyes ping-ponged between Gabby's amused smirk and my unyielding stance. The movers, caught in our personal tug-of-war, looked ready to auction off the sofa to the highest bidder and wash their hands of the whole affair.

"Are you done yet?" I asked William, growing tired of the spectacle.

"Elizabeth, just a minute," William implored, his voice cracked with urgency.

"William, there's really nothing left to say," I replied, my tone frostier than an Antarctic breeze. "I'm going home."

"But what if I have something that could change everything?" he asked, his gaze drilling into mine with a desperation I hadn't seen before.

"Unless you've got a magic wand or a time machine stashed in your back pocket, I doubt it," I scoffed, waving at the movers to resume their task. But William—oh, dear William—had other plans.

"Stop!" he bellowed, leaping onto the sofa as if mounting a steed in some absurd knightly quest. The movers halted, exchanging glances that said they'd seen it all now.

"Really, William? Sofa surfing? What's next, jousting with floor lamps?" My attempt at humor was a thin veil over my growing irritation.

He hopped down, face earnest, hands outstretched. "Elizabeth, I love you. You can't leave—not like this."

My heart hiccupped. Mad as I was, those three little words from him were like a lightning bolt to my carefully constructed defenses. But anger regained its grip swiftly. "How could you say that?"

"Because it's true," he said. "I love you. It's been a bumpy ride, but I've finally realized that's what's going on."

"Is this one of your campaign strategies?" I said, my arms crossed.

"No, no, no, listen. Since the fallout, I've been trying to piece together what matters to me." His voice softened. "And it's not the campaign, it's not winning, it's not even being right. It's you, Elizabeth. It's always been you. All the political chess, the smoke and mirrors—none of it means anything without you."

"William . . . ."

"Please," he implored, "just say you'll consider giving me another chance."

I turned to Gabby, whose eyes danced with hope and mischief. "Did you put him up to this, girlie?" She just held up her hands in defense and shook her head.

The movers, who seemed to have gotten deeply invested in our drama, offered shrugs that seemed to translate to 'Why not?'.

"Give him another chance, young lady," one of them grumbled, a smile tugging at his bearded face.

"Easy for you to say," I muttered, but inside, my resolve was melting faster than ice cream on the Fourth of July.

* * *

"Listen," William said, looking around at his audience, who seemed to be growing with nosy onlookers, "I didn't want to say it, but, I have to tell you."

"Yes," I said, still huffy.

"You might have heard that I quit the George campaign."

I glanced over to Gabby. "So I read in the paper."

He shuffled uncomfortably, casting a look at Gabby and the burly movers and a few other bystanders. "Yes," William finally said with a resolute nod. "Well the paper didn't include the reason why."

"It didn't?"

"Listen, Charlie Archer is going to run as an independent and I'm going to join his team."

I almost fell over in shock. "You're what?!"

"I'm joining his team. Charlie. Archer. And, Elizabeth," he leaned toward me, "We want you to spearhead the campaign."

The words struck like a gale force wind, blowing away the cobwebs of doubt that clung to my thoughts. All my dreams, my aspirations for change in D.C., they fluttered back into view, vibrant and somehow newly attainable.

"I . . . I can't believe it."

"Look, Peats is out," William continued, his hands gesturing with newfound fervor. "And with your talent, with your vision, we can take on George. We can do this. We can win a clean race."

One of the movers, a guy with arms like steel cables and a surprisingly contemplative brow, chimed in. "He ain't wrong. Archer's got that cross-party appeal. No mud on his boots yet."

"Thank you for the astute political commentary," I said.

"Listen to him," Gabby nudged me, her grin infectious. "And, Libby, listen to your heart."

William stepped forward, taking my hands in his. His palms were balmy, his grip firm. "What do you say, Elizabeth? One last campaign . . . for us?"

"Us," I echoed, the word tingling on my tongue. It was a gamble, a leap into the unknown. But wasn't that what life in D.C. was all about?

"Go on, girl," the mover encouraged, his eyebrow raised in anticipation.

"You know I would be crazy for even considering it," I relented, a chuckle escaping me. "But remember, 'No mud on the boots'? Let's keep it that way."

"Deal," William beamed, relief washing over him as he picked me up into a hug as he stood.

Gabby started clapping and the movers put down the sofa and joined in, followed by the other onlookers. It was a regular standing ovation as he spun me around.

I squealed into a laugh, and held his face as he put me back down and kissed me.

"Okay, boys," William said, "you know what to do."

"Yes, sir!" they said and started taking the sofa back in.

"Well Gabs," I said as we sauntered back into my apartment, "it looks like you're going to have to put up with my puns at least a little while longer."

"Girl, that's a sacrifice I'm willing to take," she said, and waved goodbye.

CHAPTER 24

AS THE CITY glittered below, its lights like a sea of stars, memories of my first arrival in Washington D.C. flooded back. The excitement, the nerves, the feeling of stepping into a new chapter of my life. And now, here I stood on top of it all in a shimmering gown, not blue, not red, but gold. It was home after all. I just didn't know it yet.

"Oh there you are," William said as strutted out to the patio with a couple of glasses of champagne. "The press want a word." He placed his hand on my back as he joined me at the rail.

"What could they possibly want from me?" I said, rolling my eyes playfully.

"I'd say, they want to hear from the brightest, most talented, most beautiful young strategist in D.C.," William specified with a smirk dancing on his lips, his eyes twinkling mischievously. "Who just pulled off the biggest underdog victory in Senate history."

I couldn't help but chuckle at his theatrics, grateful for his unwavering support amidst the chaos.

"Don't they know that I owe it all to the brightest, most amazing, handsomest young consultant in D.C.?"

"Well," he said, placing his face right next to mine, "you'll just have to remind them."

He kissed me, and then we took a moment to look out over the skyline before turning to head into the party.

Made in the USA
Monee, IL
03 June 2025

18738131R00108